COMPLACENCY

COMPLACENCY

ONE MAN'S STORY

EDWARD MINYARD

ARCHWAY
PUBLISHING

Archway Publishing books may be ordered through booksellers or by contacting:

Archway Publishing
1663 Liberty Drive
Bloomington, IN 47403
www.archwaypublishing.com
844-669-3957

ISBN: 978-1-6657-4459-1 (sc)
ISBN: 978-1-6657-4460-7 (e)

Library of Congress Control Number: 2023909541

Print information available on the last page.

Archway Publishing rev. date: 08/02/2023

CONTENTS

This book, as with all my other books, is dedicated to my darlin', Joy Tarbell. She's my best friend, my source of energy, and, lately, my nurse. She can be counted on to ask brilliant questions, purely from a place of curiosity. She's logical, and she's rational – two traits that often elude me.

I further dedicate this book to our family of seven wonderful children, their husbands, wives, significant others, and fur babies, along with our nine (so far) grandkids and two great grandkids. While all aren't named in this story, their presence is known.

ACKNOWLEDGEMENTS

Writing a novel is not a one-person job. Aside from the hundreds of social media cheerleaders, there are more than a few real-world humans who have each played important roles. My two stalwart editors, Dr. Larry Katz (also my bro-in-law and sax player extraordinaire) and Terry Mednick, my detail-oriented, logical friend. These guys have kept my grammar and punctuation in check, even against my protestations.

My best friend (and my co-author of Decisive Judgment) Roger Lee Dorethy, my reliable sounding board for plot vectors, congruity, and moral support.

John I. Mitchell, my dear friend, for pre-reading the manuscript and giving it a great review.

Finally, all my friends who loaned their names and / or personalities (knowingly or otherwise) to this story. Ron Rivera; Bobbie Dunn; Sarah Burton; Susan Hardy; Juan Godoy; Steve Thompson – thank you. (Please don't sue me).

FOREWORD

In a world where unforeseen threats constantly surface and complacency jeopardizes our safety, Edward E. Minyard's captivating novel, "Complacency: One Man's Story," serves as both an enthralling literary journey and a crucial reminder of the need for preparedness and resilience. As a former Military Intelligence Officer and, later a Chief Information Officer, I have witnessed the significance of staying vigilant and adaptive in the face of challenges.

Drawing from his wealth of real-life experience in crisis management, disaster response, and cybersecurity, Minyard crafts a gripping story of an attack on America, emphasizing the dangers of disregarding potential threats. The novel follows the protagonist, Michael Conrad, as he navigates a tumultuous world, striving to protect his family and team amid collapsing societal norms and catastrophic events. This potent narrative reveals the unsettling parallels between Minyard's fictional universe and the volatile reality we confront today.

"Complacency" goes beyond storytelling, offering an insightful tutorial on personal preparedness, empowering readers with the knowledge and skills to survive when conventional support systems fail. Including a collection of references and recommended "how-to" books, Minyard provides readers with the resources to anticipate and triumph over adverse circumstances.

Reflecting on recent incidents, such as the 2021 Texas power grid collapse — which I lived through — it becomes evident that complacency can lead to devastating outcomes. "Complacency" encourages us to question our assumptions and take proactive measures to ensure our future safety. May this novel inspire you to cultivate the spirit of resilience that lives within us all.

John I. Mitchell
Former Captain, Military Intelligence, United States Army
Former Chief Information Officer, Neiman Marcus and Melville Corporation

PREFACE

The world we live in today is a complex tapestry of interwoven challenges and opportunities. As we collectively face the reality of an ever-evolving global landscape, the significance of preparedness, adaptability, and resilience has never been more apparent. It is within this context that "Complacency" was born—a story that seeks to shed light on the fragile balance between security and vulnerability, and the consequences of inaction in the face of looming threats.

As a seasoned professional with over four decades of experience in crisis management, disaster response, risk management, and cybersecurity, I have witnessed firsthand the devastating impact of unpreparedness and complacency. Time and time again, I have seen how the consequences of these oversights reverberates through communities, nations, and indeed, the world. In writing "Complacency," my goal was to create a compelling narrative that not only entertains but also serves as a powerful reminder of the importance of vigilance and preparedness in an increasingly uncertain world.

Throughout my career, I have had the privilege of working with many organizations, both in the public and private sectors, that are dedicated to addressing the complex challenges associated with disaster response and recovery. These experiences have provided me with invaluable insights and a unique perspective on the intricacies of crisis management and the resilience of the human spirit. I have sought to weave these insights into the very fabric of "Complacency," infusing the story with a sense of realism that invites readers to confront their own assumptions and question their preparedness.

"Complacency" is, at its core, a reflection of the world we live in—a world fraught with potential threats and challenges, yet also brimming with hope, innovation, and the indomitable human spirit. Through the eyes of its characters and the unfolding of the plot, the story invites readers to consider the delicate interplay between technology and humanity and the critical need for us to remain ever vigilant and adaptable in the face of adversity.

As you embark on this literary journey, I invite you to explore the pages of "Complacency" with an open mind and a willingness to question the status quo. I hope that in doing so, you will not only find yourself immersed in an engaging and thought-provoking narrative but will also be inspired to reflect on your own role in fostering a culture of preparedness and resilience.

With warm regards,
Edward E. Minyard

PROLOGUE

Complacency. It's so comfortable. And so easy to accept. It's always there, lurking in the shadows of great successes and long periods of boredom. And complacency is not your friend.

Michael had over two decades invested in the processes of preparedness, both for him and his clients. Even longer if his military career was factored in. He made a great living, espousing the philosophy that "Preparedness is not Paranoia" and selling that philosophy to others. He believed it and convinced others to believe it, too. "Preparing for *<insert name of dreadful thing here>* is important!" he would emphatically say, pounding his fist on whatever podium he commanded.

He delivered his spiel with the passion of an expert - a guru, in fact. The Master of Disaster, they called him. Attendees to his impassioned presentations at many of the world's most prestigious conferences hustled home, eager to convince their leaders to increase their budgets—and most times, they did. Then, time passed and... nothing happened. When nothing happened, those who control the budgets saw no value in the idea of preparedness. "Statistically speaking," they would say, "if it hasn't happened to us yet, it probably won't!"

But crises don't follow statistics.

If one were to assign any type of personification to a significant crisis, it would be that a crisis loves complacency. Michael saw it over and over again. He wrote articles about the "John Wayne Syndrome"—the belief that if we admit to the dangers "out there", said admission may be viewed as an admission of fear.

Can't have that now, can we?

No one likes to think about The Big One. But, sure as the sky is blue, The Big One came along… and it was not just one thing. There were many bad things, all at once, everywhere.

People could have seen much of it coming if they'd have opened their eyes. Some of the bad things were predictable, based on the geopolitical goings-on in the country and the world. Others were decidedly unpredictable. Michael's position has always been that preparedness and predictability are not closely related. No one can make a perfect prediction about the impact or possible occurrence of any potential threat. And no preparedness plan can ever be perfect, either. "Planning is always more important than having a plan!" he would say.

The nemesis of every planner is the "C word" – complacency – and America had become the very definition of it.

CHAPTER 1

AND SO IT BEGINS

THE GATES OF Hell opened widest in 2025—as if 2023 and 2024 hadn't been bad enough. No one thought things could get much worse after '24. Much of Europe was made uninhabitable, resulting from the destruction of Ukraine's Zaporizhzhia nuclear plant. Neither warring factor admitted to the shelling, of course. Russia and Ukraine blamed each other. Not that it mattered.

"The pressure vessel of a modern reactor is very robust and can withstand considerable damage from phenomena such as earthquakes and to an extent kinetic impacts," a professor of materials physics at Imperial College London had said. "It is not designed to withstand attacks by explosive weaponry," he had added. "It seems to me unlikely that such an impact would result in a Chernobyl-like nuclear event, but this has never been tested, and it is not impossible."

Turned out it was possible. Within three days, a radioactive cloud spread over seventeen countries in the region, including Ukraine, Belarus, Moldova, Lithuania, Latvia, Estonia, Poland, Romania, Serbia, Hungary, Slovakia, the Czech Republic, Turkey, Armenia, Azerbaijan, Georgia, and Russia—rendering them unlivable for generations. Because the prevailing winds blow from west to east, Russia was most severely impacted by the radioactive plume. The entire world was impacted by the ensuing humanitarian crisis.

After the cancer-related death of Vladimir Putin, Russia was now under the leadership of Nikolai Platonovich Patrushev. Patrushev had been a close confidant of Putin. The two shared the same political ideologies and were both former spies from the days of the KGB. Patrushev served in the KGB and its successor agency, the FSB. He replaced Vladimir Putin as the head of the spy agency. The new leader, like Putin, also espoused the beliefs of Alexander III, who used to say, "Russia has only two allies—its own army and its own navy." Still, prior to his death, Putin had cemented his ties with Pyongyang and established North Korea as a fallback location for Russian government operations.

Patrushev relocated all of his top leadership there, just weeks before the devastating attacks on the Zaporizhzhia nuclear plant. Russia had other supporting nations, such as Belarus, Greece, India, Venezuela, Cuba, and—to a somewhat lesser degree—China. But none were as convenient or as willing to cooperate as North Korea. Especially China, who was actively involved in their own invasion of Taiwan. In fact, leaders in Beijing were closely watching as the Russians weakened. They had ideas of their own, or so it seemed.

2023 was the year of the Great Eastern European Exodus, spreading refugees to every other continent. Those that would accept them, that is. At first, most countries opened their arms wide for the newly countryless horde. That was before the new Covid variant that they brought spread. Variant BX6.5 was terrible. It was the most virulent strain to-date and had a forty percent mortality rate, escaping both prior natural and vaccine-induced immunity. No prior vaccine was effective against it. One new vaccine was, though.

It was developed in China, but they weren't sharing it with the rest of the world. As a result, open arms became middle fingers. Many ports of entry were closed, resulting in massive refugee camps in those countries still accepting the migrants. One of them was the United States of America.

The US-of-A was experienced in dealing with sheltering masses of people. The Federal Emergency Management Agency (FEMA), The

Office of Refugee Resettlement (ORR) and the Department of Health and Human Services (HHS) had lots of recent experience to call upon. As recently as 2022, resources were mobilized to shelter tens of thousands of Afghani Refugees—known as 'Operation Allies Welcome.' Along with the Department of Defense, the agencies also built massive Covid quarantine camps across the nation, where thousands of civilians and military waited out their Covid exposure risk periods.

ORR and partner agencies were constantly busy sheltering a steady flow of thousands of unaccompanied children, families and single adults who had crossed the southern border illegally. Yes, plenty of experience—but this new demand was overwhelming. The Great Eastern European Exodus grotesquely combined all those past programs - but on steroids.

Michael Conrad knew all there was to know about sheltering displaced human beings. Under contract to one or the other of the federal and/or state agencies responsible for such missions, he had built and operated numerous shelters, in "tent cities", modified shipping containers, abandoned big-box retail stores, warehouses, schools, stadiums—even a horserace track. Virtually any space large enough to set up enough cots for the teeming masses.

He had seen the chaos firsthand. And he had often watched as the "organized chaos" of the first few days devolved into a total chaos that inevitably grew out of the uncomfortable experience of being jammed into a space with hundreds or thousands of total strangers. But not even Michael was prepared for the challenges of this new global crisis.

Shelters tend to evolve into pseudo-communities. Like any other community, they also tend to further evolve—or devolve—into sub-communities, reflecting the characteristics of those within the shelter community. Cultures, socio-economic status, religion, gang affiliations—they all show themselves. Just like in the "real world", Michael had seen it all. It wasn't always pretty, and neither was every shelter a "safe place" for those inside it. Drugs, sexual assault, physical assault. People bring their problems with them. These problems apply no matter who the sheltered population is or where they are from—foreign or domestic. That said, when those being sheltered are also immigrants, the issues are even more challenging. Shelter operators and their supporting agencies also have to deal with the "political environment du jour" and the concerns / prejudices of those outside the shelter walls.

In 2023, the USA was a political nightmare, to say the least. Outright hatred between the members of the Republicans and Democrats led to verbal and physical confrontations across the nation. States were making their own rules regarding everything from firearm ownership to abortion laws. Many were even censoring or outright banning websites that didn't conform to the laws and regulations the State imposed.

Political extremist groups like ANTIFA and Proud Boys were engaging in armed confrontations. America was getting ever closer to a second Civil War. The immigration shelters were high-test fuel for the fires of hatred. Michael had seen it coming. His work with sheltering migrants—particularly unaccompanied children—from Central America had shown him the ugliness that people could demonstrate. Sheltering the refugees created by the Great Eastern European Exodus was even worse. The public outrage against these shelters seemed to be the one thing upon which many Americans, regardless of their political views, agreed. It started with peaceful protests, but once the new Covid variant reared its ugly head, the "protests" became violent.

CHAPTER 2

UPRISING IN NEW MEXICO

AFTER THE POLITICAL upheaval caused by the 2022 midterm elections, the United States Government was in a state of imbalance. The Democratic Party had lost control of the House of Representatives, but had retained the Senate. Passing any legislation was harder than it had ever been. The president was forced to issue more Executive Orders than at any other time in history, just to get anything accomplished. His decision to allow a United Nations contingent to open and operate shelters within the borders of the United States was one of his most unpopular, even within his own party. It was the only choice left to him.

Then, because of the nuclear plant disaster in Ukraine, NATO had no options left. The member countries had become engaged in the conflict with Russia and their allies, North Korea and Iran. The conflict had remained non-nuclear—so far—but the ground fighting was intense. In support of NATO, the USA had deployed thousands of troops to Europe. If that weren't challenge enough, because of China's aggressions in Taiwan, the US Navy and Marines had been deployed in large numbers to the Marianna's Islands and the Philippines, further depleting the troops available to deal with homeland-related issues.

Left stateside were most of the country's National Guard units— but these were controlled by state governors—not all of whom were supportive of the current political leadership in Washington, DC. Some of those governors had refused to send troops overseas or to other states, causing the president to enact Tile 10, federalizing the National Guard in several opposing states.

The language of Title 10 is clear:

> *Whenever —*
> *(1) the United States, or any of the Commonwealths or possessions, is invaded or is in danger of invasion by a foreign nation;*
> *(2) there is a rebellion or danger of a rebellion against the authority of the Government of the United States; or*
> *(3) the President is unable with the regular forces to execute the laws of the United States;*
>
> *The President may call into Federal service members and units of the National Guard of any State in such numbers as he considers necessary to repel the invasion, suppress the rebellion, or execute those laws. Orders for these purposes shall be issued through the governors of the States.*

In 2024, a case could be made that all three conditions applied. For fifty years, the military of the United States had been served by an All-Volunteer Force (AVF). Beginning in 2022, all its branches of service were failing or struggling to meet recruiting requirements. The new conflicts were not inspiring massive enlistments as had the War on Terrorism. Morale had been severely impacted after the war in Afghanistan, then strained even more by Covid vaccination requirements.

Politicians on the right and left were now calling to bring back the draft. Public unpopularity notwithstanding, the Constitution calls for the ability to raise an armed force — coercively if necessary. Two years of dealing with government mandates showed that the American public will ultimately go along with what the government dictates, though it may kick and scream along the way. The state of global affairs in 2023 and the expectations of even more geopolitical conflicts in the near future made reinstitution of the draft all but inevitable. But it would take the one commodity that no one seemed to have in 2023—time. The influx of the European refugees and the continual flow of migrants across America's southern border dictated immediate action. The United Nations was the only viable choice—or so it seemed.

The United Nations High Commission for Refugees, also known as the UN Refugee Agency, was created in 1950 to help millions of Europeans who had fled or lost their homes during the Second World War. Their current mission was to protect and assist millions of displaced and stateless people around the world. Now, seventy-three years later, in the United States of America, it was like *déjà vu* all over again. Staff and volunteers from most of the sixty-one member nations—those that weren't either at war themselves or deployed to other refugee camps— were brought to Holloman Airforce Base in Alamogordo, New Mexico.

The UN also insisted on sending a large contingent of Blue Hats— members of the UN Peacekeeping Force. They were armed. That's where things went south. For the first time since the Civil War, an armed, foreign force was operating on American soil. UN Peacekeeper Forces, until 2023, didn't exist for countries like the United States, or the other various semi-super states in the world. They existed for countries teetering on economic collapse and without clear governmental controls. States where the people are highly likely to get crushed under the weight of slow-moving political friction. In 2023, that was the United States of America. Thing was, the population is huge, inherently belligerent, occasionally xenophobic, and surprisingly well armed. The American population is notoriously argumentative among itself but pretty quick to form up into hyper-partisan solidarity when faced with an external aggressor. The decision to allow armed UN "peacekeepers" on US soil lit the fuse to a massive powder keg.

Michael had been deployed to Haiti after the massive earthquake in 2011. There, he saw firsthand how desperate people behave when they can see no brightness in their futures. He worked closely with the United Nations Stabilization Mission in Haiti (MINUSTAH)—though most Haitians referred to them as "TOURISTA". Some of Michael's Haitian crew described instances where MINUSTAH forces stood by and did nothing to stop gang-related criminal actions, acting more like people on vacation than a "peacekeeping mission".

On several humanitarian missions, Michael was assigned MINUSTAH troops to provide security. He worked with troops from several countries under stressful conditions. Some of those troops were solid operators. Some, not so much. The Jordanian troops, for example, were compassionate. The Sri Lankan contingent, fearful, and all but useless. But some — especially the Brazilian soldiers—were brutal and borderline sadistic. They all wore "Blue Hats"—helmets and berets—but they weren't all the same.

Each brought their own prejudices and geopolitical views to every mission. The UN Peacekeepers deployed to New Mexico were no different, save that many of the countries that hated either each other—or America—had either withdrawn from the United Nations Peacekeeping Mission or refused to deploy to the United States. Others declined to be deployed because the wolves were at their own doors.

The country with the largest contingent of troops seconded to the UN was Bangladesh. That had been true for over a decade. The Bangladesh Army was widely praised for their humanitarianism—and for their fighting prowess when it proved necessary. The United Nations sent 300 Bangladesh Army troops to the USA to provide security to the UN Refugee Agency personnel and those living in the new shelters. Three hundred troops with strange uniforms and big white military vehicles.

The conspiracy theorist websites had a field day with all that. Adding to the "outrage" was the fact that many of the refugees and most of the people deployed by the United Nations were followers of Islam. It was the perfect breeding ground for the fear-driven hatred of the extreme political right. And those people showed up in droves to protest outside the gates of Holloman Air Force Base.

The scenes were surrealistic. Most of the protestors and all the "defenders" were in combinations of Tyvek HazMat suits and full-on biohazard protective gear. The protestors—and their counter-protestors from the extreme left—were proudly exhibiting their second Amendment rights to bear arms. The UN Peacekeepers and United States Air Force Security Forces guards were better armed, of course, but as per most such protests, none were pointing weapons at one another. Not at first. Just waving signs, yelling chants—and the frequent incidents between the left and right in the bars of Alamogordo at the end of stressful days. Then, the pictures were leaked.

The UN flew all their people, materiel and supplies directly into the base. Refugees were brought in that way, as well. Some enterprising soul at Holloman had been regularly leaking pictures and videos to any press outlet that would publish them. Fox News, of course, and Breitbart splashed them every day.

They were informative and roused the rabble, but weren't really more than was to be expected. Until the C-5 transport plane full of "specialty trailers" arrived. Mobile crematoriums. Hundreds of them. The leaked videos showed close-up shots of these systems and even had images of the field manuals.

No unauthorized persons had been inside the base since the refugee mission had begun and although it seemed logical that many of the refugees and their caregivers must have contracted the new Covid variant, none were being transported to local or regional hospitals.

It now seemed obvious why they hadn't been. The idea of mass deaths within the confines of an American military base amplified the protests. People wanted answers: none were forthcoming. Tensions were high, and the crowds were growing. If the fuse hadn't already been burning toward the powder keg, it was then. Literally.

Local supporters of both elements of protestors had been making daily deliveries of food and water to the protest site. Cases of water and MREs were stacked near the fences of the base, and folks could help themselves. On one morning, one of the MRE cases was marked with a small, red smear of paint. Only one man noticed it, though. He was in a truck, a quarter mile away, looking through a rifle scope. Only he knew that the marked box was filled with pre-mixed Tannerite. Tannerite was a legal and highly stable compound used in shooting practices. Stable, until the two-element combination of oxidizers and aluminum powder is mixed by the user, then shot by a high-velocity bullet.

The man in the truck took careful aim, fired, and watched as the twenty-five pounds of powder exploded. The blast was massive. Five people were killed instantly. Many more were wounded by flying debris or badly burned by the explosion. The protestors were shocked into a stunned silence. But the UN and Air Force guards reacted differently. Believing that they were under attack, the UN Peacekeepers opened fire on the crowds outside the wire, killing or wounding dozens of civilians. The Air Force troops turned their weapons on the still-shooting UN troops, killing several of them before a ceasefire order was given. The shit had hit the proverbial fan.

"The Tannerite Massacre", as it was later called, was the catalyst for the New Mexico uprising, but what happened next was worse. Hearing the explosion and gunshots, the refugees inside the compound—most having only recently escaped ground zero for what was devolving into World War III—rioted. Like every community, leaders had arisen among the ranks of the refugees. Rumors and misinformation were more available than truths inside the compound, and these new "leaders" took advantage of the lack of facts to gain control over the population.

It hadn't been difficult. People were disappearing every day, ostensibly being sent to hospitals for treatment of Covid BX6.5. None were returned. The ones taking charge told the crowds about the mobile crematoriums and that they were part of a plot to exterminate all the refugees. When the explosion happened, followed by the sounds of machine guns firing and people screaming, thousands of those held in the camp charged for the massive hole left in the perimeter fence, breaking their way to what they perceived as freedom.

Some were shot by the surviving civilians outside the wire. Some were shot by troops from inside the wire. Some grabbed guns from the dead and wounded and shot back. The massive herd of humanity kept moving, though, straight towards the small town of Alamogordo, where they forced their way into buildings and homes.

Many stole cars and trucks and drove away into the mountains and deserts of New Mexico, focused only on escaping what they were sure would have been their mass annihilation at the hands of the United Nations or the Americans outside the fences of the refugee camp.

CHAPTER 3

FORT BLISS SHELTER

AT THE TIME of the events in New Mexico, Michael Conrad was working one hundred miles south at Fort Bliss, Texas. He was assigned to manage and operate an Influx Shelter, the newly coined term for detainment centers operated by the Office of Refugee Resettlement— housing almost 10,000 undocumented aliens from Central and South America and over 100 other nations.

The site at Fort Bliss was the largest such facility in the country but not the only one. The flow of migrants across the Rio Grande River had been steadily increasing since Michael first became involved in building these facilities back in 2014. In Fiscal Year 2020, there were over 440,000 migrant encounters at the southern border. In Fiscal Year 2021, the number increased to over 1.5 million. By 2022, the number increased to over 2.2 million undocumented aliens, encountered and processed by US Customs and Border Protection.

The Influx Shelter concept, by any name, was unpopular on both sides of the political aisle. It always had been so through three different presidents. The only thing that had changed for Michael and his teams during all those years was which political camp hated them, and which looked at them as "humanitarians". And the costs, of course: they kept increasing. Each person housed in these facilities cost the American Taxpayer over $700 per night for care, feeding, clothes, healthcare, education, legal services, counseling, and all the infrastructure required to support the facilities.

The right wing screamed about the costs while the left wing screamed about "kids in cages". Michael and his team just kept their heads in the game and did their job.

The events in New Mexico changed everything. Every cellphone within the shelter complex began chirping. The distinct sound was a special warning tone, determined by Michael Conrad as a part of his mass notification system. This system sent instantaneous alerts to his entire database of employers, employees, and partners via text messages, emails and automated phone messages, informing them of an emergency and giving them further instructions. The message was ominous:

THIS IS NOT A DRILL—LOCK DOWN, LOCK DOWN, LOCK DOWN—THIS IS NOT A DRILL

It was Michael's job as Operations Manager to approve any and all mass notification messages. Emergency messages such as this required Michael to approve transmission by entering a PIN number on his iPhone. He had not approved this broadcast message—and he had not authorized it.

"Rivera!" Michael yelled to his Chief Technology Officer. "MassBlast has been compromised! Get me detai…"

Michael hadn't finished his sentence when loudspeakers around the entire facility of Fort Bliss began wailing. Everyone working within the confines of the base had been trained on the meaning of all the daily sounds of Reveille, Retreat, Taps and the myriad of other daily bugle calls, and what to do when they sounded. This wasn't one of them. This one was a fright-inducing wavering howl, screaming out in a non-stop series of five-minute blasts. Everyone had been trained on this one, too:

3-5 MINUTE WAVERING TONE ON SIREN: AN ATTACK/HOSTILE ACT IS IMMINENT OR IN PROGRESS

- BE ALERT, ENSURE ALL PERSONNEL ARE WARNED
- IMPLEMENT SECURITY MEASURES AS APPROPRIATE
- FOLLOW INSTRUCTIONS TO TAKE COVER, EVACUATE TO A SAFE LOCATION OR SHELTER
- CONDUCT PERSONNEL ACCOUNTABLITY

Michael's radio went crazy. Every gate, guard station, and operations supervisor, all wanted to know the same thing: "What the fuck is going on?" He keyed his mic and shouted, "STOP! RADIO DISCIPLINE, NOW!" The chatter stopped. Michael keyed his mic again and spoke calmly, "All hands, all hands. This is Eagle One. We are all aware of what is currently going on, but we do not know exactly why. Your orders are to follow the prescribed protocols and procedures for the emergency directives that have been issued. Just do your jobs. If you are not directly involved with security or operations, shelter in place. More information will be provided as we discover it. Eagle One, out."

Turning back to his Chief Tech, Michael said, "Ron, what do you have for me? Who sent that message? Have we been hacked? Any alerts from the SolarWinds systems?"

Rivera looked up from his triple-monitor display. "SolarWinds is offline, sir. So are the firewalls. We are unable to restart them at this time. Still on it, sir."

SolarWinds was the best security event management solution on the market, as were the Barracuda firewalls. These systems had successfully detected and blocked thousands of attacks on Michael's systems over the past years. Lately, particularly since the escalation of the war in Europe, the attacks were closer to a thousand per week. Michael's intrusion detection and firewall systems needed to be right every time. The bad actors, though, only needed to be right one time like they had been that day. But what about the general emergency alert from the base? Had the entire base IT infrastructure been successfully penetrated? Michael's cellphone rang. It was the Base Commander's Office.

"Michael Conrad, hold for General Prescott," said the caller. Lieutenant General John Prescott and Lieutenant Colonel Michael Conrad (Retired) had served together for decades. Both graduates of the same class at "The Benning School for Boys"—also known as Airborne Ranger School at Fort Benning, Georgia—they were quick to become lifelong friends. And they both fit the old description of men such as they:

> *A difficult child at best, fit neither for the cloth nor the pen, too dangerous to be unleashed upon society and too horrible to let live, but yet too brilliant and unique to destroy; He was eventually given over to The Fort Benning School For Boys to receive the proper education and be brought up right as both a savior and destroyer of man.*

They had served together in Grenada, Panama, Kosovo, Somalia, Iraq, and Afghanistan. Michael was now a civilian contractor working an unpopular mission, forced upon General Prescott by an even less popular Federal Agency. And now, this new shitstorm. Their friendship was strong, but this was strictly business.

"Conrad, what the everlovin' fuck is happening on my goddam base?" Prescot asked. His voice was calm but his tone was anything but. "Who sent that comms blast, and who in the name of George fucking Bush authorized the use of my emergency broadcast systems?"

"Sir, we are investigating now," Michael replied. We have no visibility into your alert system, though. What is obvious is, this has all the earmarks of a coordinated attack. I will keep you informed as our investigation evolves."

Softening his tone, General Prescott said, "Mike, I don't feel good about this. First, that fiasco up the road at Holloman, now strange happenings here. Somebody is stirring the shit."

"I feel the same way, John," Michael ensured. "Our systems are locked down tight, yet someone managed to crack the code. We aren't seeing any indications that data was exfiltrated. They created a bit of havoc with their broadcast message, which is a nuisance, but no serious harm—this time. We're working to determine if they left behind a 'backdoor' for more nefarious actions later."

Conrad was still on the phone with Prescott when the second alert came over MassBlast:

FIRE; FIRE; FIRE—THIS IS NOT A DRILL—FIRE, FIRE, FIRE DETECTED IN DORMS A, B, C, AND D—EVACUATE! EVACUATE! EVACUATE! REPORT IMMEDIATELY TO DESIGNATED MUSTER POINTS!

"John, are you seeing this?" Michael asked. "I can't believe it's genuine, but we have to treat it like it is. Will your firefighters respond while under a general lockdown? This will be a real clusterfuck, sir... more so if it's the real deal."

"I got the MassBlast, and I'm sure the Fire Chief did, too. Still, I'll call him myself. Prescott out," the General said, ending the call with Michael.

"Rivera!" Conrad yelled. "I need answers, and I need them right fucking now! What's going on here?

"Sir," Rivera replied, "it appears that the hack is through the actual cloud-based server. The bad actors are in control of MassBlast, and we are locked out. This could get worse before it gets better. As you are aware, the system can be programmed to send either pre-established or ad hoc messages to any phone numbers and/or email addresses in or added to the database. The operative word being 'any.' Remember the false alarm sent to every resident of Hawaii back in 2018? Everyone thought they had less than twenty minutes to find shelters. It created mass pandemonium. Our system could be used that way, sir. At this time, I have no way of stopping them. As of right now, they only appear to be sending our canned messages to our predefined user group. We have no way of knowing if anything broader is happening."

"Holy fucking shit," was all Michael Conrad could say. Michael dialed the number on his encrypted WhatsApp system for his Contracting Officer at ORR. Dave Ellis was top of Michael's chain of command, but this needed to be escalated much higher than the Office of Refugee Resettlement. This problem could quickly become one with national defense implications.

Ellis' response was the same as Michael's had been. "Holy fucking shit!" he said. "I'm walking this up the ladder. Stay tuned for further actions."

While the broader implications were clear, Michael had always subscribed to Smokey the Bear's First Rule of Emergency Management: "When stomping out forest fires, get those closest to your ass first!" Right now, Michael had a genuine fire alarm to deal with, and it was damn close to his ass.

When he arrived at the first Muster Point, Michael was not surprised. His teams were well-practiced at fire evacuations because he'd insisted on monthly drills. The situation was less-than-orderly but was being managed. As well as any fire drill involving thousands of people could ever be managed, that is. The usual amount of yelling, laughing, and mischief was in play, but Michael's team was handling the situation. Looking not so jovial were Lt. General John Prescott and his Fire Chief, Col. Calvin Brown. Michael had met Col. Brown in a few planning meetings, but the man was not smiling now.

"First things first, Mr. Conrad. There is no fire," Col. Brown stated. "Next, what kind of piece of shit system are you operating over there? We are in a base-wide emergency lockdown, and you roll my teams out for a false alarm? You understand this is gonna create a tsunami of downhill rolling shit, right? I want a full incident report, A-S-A-fucking-P! Are we clear?"

"Crystal, sir," Conrad replied. "My teams can detect what happened but aren't yet clear exactly HOW it occurred. Reports will be provided to you and the rest of the organization as soon as we can reasonably and accurately generate them." Turning to the general, he continued, "Now, by your leave, sir, I have a cluster to un-fuck over here. I'll report as soon as I can."

That's when things went south.

As the men were talking, shouts rose from the crowd of detainees. Large groups from each muster group charged at the collection of firefighters and unarmed security personnel. Many of the migrants had makeshift weapons, including "shivs" and an assortment of clubs. Michael saw several of his people go down, along with some of the firefighters, standing near their vehicles.

One group of the detainees ran toward Michael and the two Army officers, obviously intending to take them out. The General's two personal security detail troopers stepped between him and the charging crowd, drawing their Sig Sauer M-17 9mm pistols, shouting, 'Halt! Halt! Halt!' The crowd did not halt. The troopers opened fire, dropping the first ranks of the attacking group. But there were just too many of them. They kept charging.

Michael, General Prescott and Col. Brown ran behind the nearest firetruck to take up a defensive position. As they ran, Brown was on his radio screaming, "Man the monitors! Man the monitors! Suppress this crowd!"

Michael didn't understand. What the fuck, he thought - monitors? He wasn't aware that "monitors" are what he understood to be "water cannons". The truck they'd run behind had one mounted on the top of it.

"On it, sir!" came the response over the radio.

Michael heard the massive pumps of the truck fire up, then heard screaming from the crowd as the high-velocity stream of water knocked them to the ground. General Prescott was also on his radio, calling for a rapid response backup unit. Michael heard *matarlos a todos!* and turned to encounter four men charging at them with makeshift weapons held high. That the attackers were shouting, "Kill them all!" set the tone for Michael's reaction.

As the first of the detainees swung a three-foot length of two-by-four at the general's head, Michael stepped in front of the man, deflecting the blow with his right hand. He then grabbed the attacking man's wrist and spun him through a 180-degree arc, slamming him into two of the other attackers. As the man made contact, Michael slammed his left forearm into the attacker's twisted arm just above the elbow.

He heard a satisfying "POP!" as the man's arm broke from the force of the strike. Turning his attention to the next two men, who were off balance from the collision with their *compadre*, Michael delivered a perfect front kick to the groin of the first one, then a solid throat punch to the second.

The fourth attacker dodged past Michael's spinning sidekick and landed a solid punch to the general's ribs. Prescott turned into the blow, striking the man in the jaw with his handheld radio. The attacker dropped where he stood.

"Rangers Lead The Way!" Michael said, giving General Prescott a fist bump.

"All the fucking way!" Prescott replied, grinning broadly. "Now, let's get the hell out of here!"

CHAPTER 4

PYONGYANG

THE MONTHLY MEETING between Sergei Alexandrovich, the new head of the Russian FSB Operational Information and International Relations Service (Fifth Service) and Won Lee Park, head of North Korea's Reconnaissance Bureau of the General Staff Department (RGB) was going well. Ironically, because both men were more fluent in English than in the other's native tongue, the meetings between the men were conducted in the language of their most significant enemy—America. That enemy was the prime topic of this meeting and most other meetings between the two spymasters because bringing America to her knees was their prime directive. And they both felt that this goal was within reach now.

"How many agents do you have inside their borders?" asked Park. "Are you in a position for large-scale actions?"

Sergei replied, "Thanks to the gracious humanitarian actions of the USA, bringing tens of thousands of Afghanis and tens of thousands of Eastern European Refugees—most with little to no background vetting—we have been able to significantly increase our skilled operators within their borders. We have been filtering vast numbers across their porous southern border for years. Over 500,000 since 2019 alone. The Mexican Cartels, as filthy as they are to deal with, have been quite helpful in our efforts to get the people securely across, and continue to smuggle in the weapons we will need. We now have a force of over one million inside the United States. In addition, we have recruited well-placed Americans across a range of Government and Private Sector entities. Our excellent provocateurs have duped both left- and right-wing Americans into doing our work for us. We have training centers in five different states, most posing as religious enclaves or other such fringe groups. We have infiltrated radical groups on both the left and the right—ANTIFA and the relatively new right-wing group that formed from the remnants of the Proud Boys and Oath Keepers, called "POK" for Proud Oath Keepers—and are fueling their hatred for each other. We have extensive plans in place for direct action, subversive action, and for sabotage. My friend, we could not be more ready!"

"Hullyunghan!" Park exclaimed, dropping into his native language. "Oh, I'm sorry—excellent!" he corrected himself. "We, too, have been making much progress! As I've informed you, my Cyber Force now has over 8,000 expert hackers. Many of them are inside the USA. We are also working closely with our friends in Iran, who have another 2,000, plus your own corps of a few thousand. Ours are better, of course, than the Iranians. But we are coordinated. The Iranians are constantly scouring the internet for vulnerabilities. Sometimes they then simply attack what they've found, locking up systems with ransomware attacks or bringing them down with distributed denial of service attacks. Vulnerabilities of more significant systems, they pass on to us."

Park continued, "We have recently had success with a small company that contracts to the American government, housing and accounting for refugees. Their data is intriguing, but their systems are more so. Especially a particular system that provides for mass notifications."

"Why is such a system valuable to our mission? Sergei asked.

Smiling, Park replied, "In 2018, a ballistic missile alert was accidentally issued via the Emergency Alert System and Wireless Emergency Alert System over television, radio, and cellphones in the American state of Hawaii. The alert stated that there was an incoming ballistic missile threat inbound to Hawaii, advised residents to seek shelter, and concluded wit: 'This is not a drill'. They all thought it was an attack by the Democratic People's Republic of Korea! Oh, we certainly could have fired such missiles, but we had not."

Park continued, "Regardless, there was chaos in their streets! No one knew what to do or where to go! A retraction wasn't sent for over half an hour. We all got a big laugh from the whole episode, but my own Directive was quite excited by the possibilities of such a system. We began to work on developing a clone and did accomplish that. We then tried marketing it through a shell company in the USA, but with little success. Until, that is, we were approached at a trade show about 'white labeling' the internals of the system to a small government contractor. They achieved great success with integrating their own enrollment and accountability solution with our mass notification system, which they call "MassBlast." They have some very smart programmers, according to our agents, but not as sophisticated as our own. We buried an actual user account into the code of the system, with full administrator permissions. We were also able to arrange for one of our own programmers to be hired by the company. While the company was well-protected from outside attackers, we simply walked in our backdoor with full accessibility rights! Once in, our cyber warriors downloaded all the target's user data, loaded it all onto our own clone of their system, then temporarily killed all of their own access to the system. We've also sent a couple of test messages, which our internal agent reported as successful. We have bigger and immediate plans for using this system now that we've stolen thousands of private, government and military credentials—personal and professional email addresses, home address, cellphone numbers. Our teams are mining those accounts, identifying our best ways to use what we learn to create problems for the American government. We already have many ideas!"

"That is interesting," Sergei remarked. "I can envision many possibilities now that I better understand the potential! I'd like to see a demonstration. I love the idea of having some fun while we work!" Before assuming command of the Russian Fifth Service, he had been the leader of the "Sandworm Team" — also known as Unit 74455 — a cyber-military unit of the GRU. The team had been behind the December 2015 Ukraine power grid cyberattack, the 2017 cyberattacks on Ukraine using the Petya malware, and the cyberattack on the Seoul 2018 Winter Olympics opening ceremony. Sergei was careful about mentioning that last thing to Park but was sure that he already suspected it. Nevertheless, Sergei loved all things cyber.

"We have something planned for tomorrow," Park said. "We need to move quickly before the American NSA and Cyber Command thwart us. It would not be easy for them—we've been planning this for years—but it won't take them long to realize the possibilities. Thanks to your own efforts in infiltrating the militant groups on both the extreme right and extreme left, we have all the data we need to stir up some trouble. That's our next step."

Sergei and his Fifth Service operatives had, indeed, been successful in not only infiltrating both sides of the American extremist camps, but in gaining leadership positions within them. ANTIFA was the more challenging of the groups. While well-organized, they are also quite decentralized in their chapters. The chapters were intentionally kept small, to reduce the risk of infiltration or having their members "outed". Still, Sergei's agents had engineered their way into ANTIFA groups in several large cities. They had organized and led several direct-action campaigns that had given them respect and notoriety through the communications back-channels of the movement.

The right-wing groups were easier, especially after the "January 6th Uprising", as it is known, which led to the conviction of the leaders of Proud Boys and Oath Keepers of seditious conspiracy. These groups and others like them required only a loud, neo-fascist, misogynist, usually white, strongman to influence them. The Proud Boys, though, had been led by one of Sergei's own people for years. A black Cuban, in fact.

The man's charisma and apparent devotion to the alternative right had been convincing enough to win over even most of the white supremacists in the group. The man had been well-trained and well-educated and had proven that, as the Americans say, you can "baffle them with bullshit". He had also won the trust of Elmer Stewart Rhodes, a lawyer and former paratrooper who was the founder of the Oath Keepers. Both of the two leaders were now serving prison sentences.

Proud Oath Keepers—the new organization formed in the wake of the trials and convictions related to the January 6^{th'} hearings and trails— now included members of Sergei's Fifth Service in chapters across the United States. Up until 2023, the groups had been mostly passive, a few instances of violence notwithstanding. They had not been overtly militant to the point of armed and deadly confrontations. But the outcome of the so-called January 6th trials, the 2022 mid-term elections and the direction of the American political landscape changed all that. POK had risen to become the face of the alt-right movement and their tactics had become more violent.

Many of the members of POK were former military and were combat tested. Some were still in the military. In 2023, POK established a strong intelligence gathering arm and used what they learned about their sworn enemies — ANTIFA in particular — to launch deadly attacks and outright assassinations against them. Much of the intelligence was "leaked" to POK from Fifth Service operatives embedded inside ANTIFA cells.

ANTIFA also stepped up their activities in 2023. Never shy about violent demonstrations, ANTIFA direct actions began to include the use of weapons they had previously only brandished. Sniper attacks were their primary methods of attack, but there had been several all-out gunfights between them and POK groups, as well. Like POK, some members of ANTIFA were former military.

Others had as far back as 2017 traveled to Syria to train and fight with the Democratic Union Party (PYD), a Kurdish nationalist group linked to the Kurdistan Workers Party (PKK)—a US- and Turkish-designated terrorist group. Most of their membership, though, were kids that had no combat experience and were more mouth than muscle. They were little more than black-clad silhouette targets for the more experienced shooters of POK. All of which played perfectly for Sergei Alexandrovich and the goals of his Fifth Service organization.

Sergei's goal was to make half of America hate the other half, sew distrust in their government, and to bring America to the brink of a new civil war and then push them over that brink. All without any overt involvement of troops from Russia or her allies—at least not in the beginning. On his right breast, Sergei had a tattoo of the words of Nikita Sergeyevich Khrushchev: *Мы вас похороним!*—"We shall bury you!"

Khrushchev made this comment during a speech on November 18, 1956. First Secretary Khrushchev said, "About the capitalist states, it doesn't depend on you whether we exist. If you don't like us, don't accept our invitations, and don't invite us to come to see you. Whether you like it or not, history is on our side. We will bury you!"

Sergei's father had been a staunch supporter of the policies and beliefs of the First Secretary and had passed his beliefs on, as had many of what was known as the "Children of Twentieth Congress". These were those who took up the reins of power under the leadership of Mikhail Gorbachev and his colleagues. The Khrushchev era provided this second generation of reformers with both an inspiration, a cautionary tale—and a genuine hatred of the West. Now, Sergei was in a position to do more than simply rage against the American Machine and her policies, and he intended to do so.

CHAPTER 5

CYBER SECURITY

"SIR," RON RIVERA began, "we have regained control of MassBlast. We were locked out from 0909 hours yesterday through 1948 hours today. Almost thirty-four hours. We had no ransom requests. All we saw when trying to access the system was that stupid fucking meme of the programmer in Jurassic Park, wagging his finger and saying, 'no, no, no!' At least the pricks could have come out of the freakin' eighties with their bullshit. We took all the right steps. We isolated the servers, documented everything, and prepared reports for you to submit. We've engaged IP Architects, who are doing deep forensics right now. As it stands—and as I told you—we have access to the system. We just don't trust it yet."

"Very well, Ron," Michael replied. "Keep doing what you're doing and keep me informed as things progress. For now, we have to assume that MassBlast is further compromised. Have IP Architects focus on whether any data was exfiltrated, modified or injected. We have a lot of PII in that database."

Michael's bosses in Washington, DC would not be happy about a breach of PII—Personal Identifiable Information—of thousands of federal employee and contractors. All of Michael's systems had passed rigorous evaluations by government investigatory agencies, testing the three most important elements of any important database: Confidentiality, Integrity, and Availability.

The CIA was the basis for everything in his world, and he did everything he could to ensure his system not only met but exceeded the standards of performance required by the government. Still, shit happened. No company or agency is immune, as was proven by the breach of the Office of Personnel Management systems back in 2015. Approximately 22.1 million records were affected, including records related to government employees, other people who had undergone background checks, and their friends and families. But that was then, and this is now. No one he reported to would give a rat's ass about something that happened while most of them were still in school. What he needed to know right now was, "how fucked are we?" He called his lead developer, Raúl Hernandez.

"Raúl, what have you got for me? First, how could this happen? Next, how bad is it, and is the system now secure?" Michael was cordial, but firm. "Come see me, ASAP."

Raúl Hernandez had been the chief developer for the Disadvantaged Business Enterprise start-up, which had developed the system Michael had dubbed MassBlast. Raúl was a first generation Cuban American, whose family had been forced out of their positions of wealth and power when Fidel Castro hijacked the island nation in 1959.

Because Raúl's father had been a close friend and schoolmate of Fidel's brother—Raúl had actually been named after Raúl Castro—the Hernandez family had been allowed to leave Cuba with some dignity and a small amount of their wealth. A better fare than most. Raúl attended Boston College, earning master's degrees in both Electrical Engineering and Systems Engineering. He was an outstanding software developer with an impressive resume, including positions with defense contractors Raytheon and Unisys, along with Deloitte, Haskins & Sells, one of the former "Big Eight" accounting firms. He was also an agent for the Democratic People's Republic of Korea.

Raúl had been recruited during his college years by a beautiful Korean woman in his Systems Engineering program. Like many impressionable college students in the 1970s, he was enamored by the Power to the People ideologies of revolutionaries, including those that had upset everything his own family had worked for.

It was not difficult for the lovely Chae-Yeong Lee to convince him that he could help right the wrongs done to his people by the Capitalists. After all, Che Guevara, then a Cuban government minister, had visited North Korea in 1960 and proclaimed it a model for Cuba to follow. In 1968, Raúl Castro stated their views were "completely identical on everything". How much more revolutionary could one get? Raúl was all in—as long as his family didn't find out, of course.

Over the next three decades, he had provided meaningful intelligence to his DPRK handlers on defense technologies, thanks to Raytheon and Unisys - financial, transportation and power grid systems - and to his involvement in the management consulting world. In his current role, Raúl was helping to engineer the social disruption of the United States or America, and he was thrilled to be a part of it.

"Raúl," Michael began, "I need a no bullshit answer from you. Did you and your developers leave any backdoors into the core of MassBlast? If so, tell me. Right fucking now."

In the world of cybersecurity, a "backdoor" refers to any method by which, authorized and unauthorized users are able to get around normal security measures and gain high-level user access (aka root access) to a computer system, network, or software application. Cybercriminals can use a backdoor to steal personal and financial data, install additional malware, and hijack devices. But backdoors aren't just for bad guys. Backdoors can also be—and often are—installed by software or hardware makers as a deliberate means of gaining access to their technology after the fact.

Backdoors of the non-criminal variety are useful for helping customers who are hopelessly locked out of their devices or for troubleshooting and resolving software issues. The current problem screamed "backdoor access" to Michael since all of his proven and expensive deterrents had been defeated without leaving a trace.

Raúl leaned forward, looking directly into Michael's eyes. "Boss, you know that's how we all work, right? Developers leave backdoors. It's expected."

"Yes, well, it's also expected that you inform your fucking boss, especially when your boss owns the fucking company!" Conrad was furious. "We've got to report this to the HHS Office of the Chief Information Officer. I expect that this little 'revelation' might cost us our FISMA and FedRamp certifications."

Adherence to FISMA—Federal Information Security Management Act—standards is required for federal agencies, departments, and contractors engaged in the processing or storage of federal data, whether a cloud service provider or not. Because Michael's company, ResourceOne, did host their data in the cloud, they were also subject to the standards of FedRAMP, the acronym for Federal Risk and Authorization Management Program. Neither certification was easy to get, and both were critical to the business.

"Michael, chill, man," Raúl said. "Those backdoors were closed before the fed investigators scoped us out. We would never have passed the sniff test if they'd still been in place—those guys are good. Clearly, you're wound up over this shit, but please don't insult my intelligence!"

Michael took a long, slow breath. He trusted Raúl. He agreed that such an obvious gap would have been discovered during the certification process, but nothing else made sense to him.

"I know," Michael said. "I apologize. You're right, of course. Not only about the backdoor but about my current stress level. I'm getting too old for this shit. I want you working with Ron Rivera and John Pironti from IP Architects to get this figured out. You can expect we will soon have a gaggle of federal forensics people involved, too. I'll keep them at bay for as long as I can. I want frequent reports. Get busy."

Too easy, thought Raúl as he left Conrad's office. He hadn't lied to the man, though. Michael was a brilliant leader and could read an outright lie at 200 meters. No, Raúl had told the truth—he just didn't tell the whole story. Yes, there had been a backdoor. Yes, he had closed that loophole before the federal certification inspection.

What he hadn't told his "boss" was that he had reopened that portal to hell, for just the briefest time, to allow his friends at the RGB to do their dirty work. Now, he would be leading the forensics investigation into his own nefarious act. Perfect, he thought. Although this guy Pironti was supposedly good. He was an internationally known expert and had a reputation for finding the fly shit in the pepper, as per the old American idiom.

Raúl had to keep his guard up, but he had refined that art over thirty years of espionage and subterfuge. He laughed to himself about the "Easter-egg" clue he'd left behind though. He'd taken the system down at 0909 hours and had allowed it to be recovered at 1948 hours. The Democratic People's Republic of Korea was founded on September 9th, 1948. Man, he thought, I crack myself up!

Then, he sneezed.

The day after the cyber "event" — Michael chose that designation because calling the disruption an "incident" carried more stringent reporting requirements, and he did not have evidence of anything worse than a lack of system availability—he got good news… and not so good news.

His first call was from General Prescott. He told Michael that the "Lock Down" alarm at Fort Bliss resulted from one of his senior staff's over-reactions to the alert sent from Michael's MassBlast system. The staff member had no authorization to send the message, but it had been done.

Prescott was handling the issue internally, and no blame was being placed on Michael. The second call was from his Contract Officer at ORR. While the folks in DC were 'concerned' about the disruption of the MassBlast system, they had bigger fish to fry. The incident at Holloman Air Force Base was dominating their limited resources. The bad news call was from John Pironti. Michael had known John for decades and was confident that if anyone could figure this shit out, he was the guy.

"Michael," John began, "I may be about to ruin your day. We are only just starting the forensic analysis—as you know, these things can take some time—but our initial review of your logs points to a probable insider threat situation. Your intrusion detection systems show nothing unexpected. Clearly, you are under a constant barrage of attempted attacks, but all seem to have been blocked. What we have found, though, is an admin account that has been activated then deactivated several times. It's like a ghost account—it's there, then it isn't. When it is there, it has unfettered access to every function of the system. Thing is, it can't deactivate and reactivate itself; someone with super admin rights has to do that."

"Sonofabitch," Michael said. "We only have three people with those rights. Myself, Ron Rivera, and Raúl Hernandez. It sure as hell wasn't me, and I've known Ron for forty years."

"My thoughts, exactly," John continued. "Raúl has been working alongside Rivera and me to investigate this event. I'm virtual, of course, but we've had Zoom calls twice daily. He has clearly deflected some of our questions. I don't have enough evidence to call him out yet, but I'd recommend removing super admin rights for both him and Rivera until further notice. And I'd start paying close attention to his work."

"Any evidence of this 'ghost' exfiltrating our data?" Michael asked.

"Not at this time," Pironti answered. "Our investigation is still ongoing. All we know right now is what you know—the system was compromised, resulting in two instances of misuse—your unauthorized broadcast messages and a period of locked availability. We can't yet determine what happened within your cloud servers during the lockout period, but we're working it."

Michael ended the call with John Pironti, then sent a Signal message to Ron Rivera, asking him to come to his office immediately. Michael's crisis management protocol required the use of the Signal encrypted messaging platform for out-of-band communications when things went sideways. Communications on Signal are end-to-end encrypted, which means only the people in messages can see the content of those messages. Based on the current situation, Michael trusted none of his internal systems at this point in time. He sent a similar message to Raúl Hernandez. Ron replied immediately that he was on his way. Raúl did not reply at all.

Raúl had a rough night. His sneezing turned to coughing. He hadn't slept well because he felt a bit feverish. When he woke up, his throat scratchy, as if he'd swallowed razor blades. Fuck me, he thought, not now! I don't have time for this bullshit! From his medicine cabinet, he took out a Covid PCR test kit—something that everyone kept on hand these days.

The Influx Shelter at Fort Bliss required testing every three days by their on-staff nurses, and he had tested negative only two days ago. But this day, he tested positive almost instantly. "Fuck me," he said, this time out loud. He swallowed two Extra-Strength Tylenol caplets and climbed back into his bed. By noon, his temperature was raging, and his breathing was difficult. He dialed 911. "I need an ambulance," was all he could rasp to the operator.

Ron Rivera had only just arrived when Michael's cellphone rang. It was the Base Hospital calling.

"Sir, we have admitted one of your employees for a Covid infection. Raúl Hernandez. He is currently unconscious and will require ventilation. We have not been able to ask him about his recent contacts, so need your input to trace them. When did you see him last?"

"Oh, man," Michel replied. "Yesterday, in my office. My very compact office. After our meeting, he was working with others on my team, in another small space. What do we need to do right now?" he asked.

Then, Michael sneezed.

CHAPTER 6

RETIREMENT

MICHAEL HEARD THE sound before he could open his eyes. *Beep, beep, beep.* A familiar sound he should have recognized, but his mind couldn't settle on what it was. *Beep, beep, beep.* Steady, slow—*beep, beep, beep.* He willed his eyes open. He was in a hospital room. He was hearing the sound was his heartbeat monitor, connected to the clamp-like probe attached to his right pointer finger. He thought, what the fuck? Then drifted back into a state of semiconsciousness.

"Mr. Conrad?" he heard the voice as if it was coming from the end of a tunnel. "Mr. Conrad, we need you to wake up, sir. Please open your eyes."

Michael opened his left eye, then his right. The room was bright. He could see two people dressed in white coveralls—no, he thought, Tyvek—wearing respirators and eye protection. One was standing next to his bed, rubbing his chest, telling him to "wake up!" The other was at the machines on the right side of his bed. Michael was confused. He wanted to ask questions, but he couldn't find his voice. He heard the *Beep, beep, beep* from the monitor grow faster.

"Easy, buddy," said the person at his bedside. Obviously, a male voice, but it was impossible to tell because of their garb. "You're fine. You are in the base hospital at Fort Bliss. You've been here for just over three weeks. Probably be with us for a while longer. I'm David, your day-shift nurse. Once you're a bit more with it, the doctor will stop by to give you all the details. For now, we need to get you up and moving. Think you can handle that?"

Michael wasn't sure what he could handle. Lifting his arm was like lifting a fifty-pound dumbbell. He tried to answer, but no words came out. He pointed to his throat. The nurse put a moisture-soaked swap to Michael's lips, telling him to suck on it.

"You probably don't want to try drinking just yet," David said. "Your throat is going to be raw for a while. These lollipop swabs will help with that. Don't worry, we're giving you plenty of fluid through your IV, so you won't get dehydrated."

A tall man walked into the room, dressed in the same protective outfits as the two nurses. "Well, good morning, sleeping beauty!" the man said. "Welcome back to the land of the living—if you can call it that. Frankly, I'd rather be asleep and dreaming than dealing with our new realities. I'm Doctor Katz. You can call me Larry. Or Doc. Or whatever. Before I let you out of here, you'll probably come up with a few other names for me—which is also cool. Don't try to talk, but let's see if you can respond to a few easy questions. Do you know what day it is?"

Michael shook his head. "That's okay—me neither," the doctor joked. "Do you remember coming to the hospital?"

Michael thought about the question. He tried to recall the last thing he remembered before waking up here. He remembered being in his office... things were blurry after that. He shook his head again.

"Let me fill in the blanks as much as I can," said Dr. Katz. "Our reports say that you walked into the Covid test center on a Friday morning three weeks ago, indicating that you had started sneezing a couple of hours prior and felt feverish. You tested positive, so were transported here for isolation and observation. As with almost every case of this new BX6.5 variant, you experienced what we're calling "Covid Crash" almost immediately. The respiratory system is attacked by the disease and then from within itself, with a cytokine storm. That means your body has gone into overdrive to fight off the virus, but with no controls on its own response. This variant, unlike previous ones, seems to cause cytokine storms right out of the gate. We think that's why the death rate is so high. The fact that you are in excellent health and are physically fit—even though you probably don't feel that way right now—is likely why you woke up 'still not dead again' today, as Willie Nelson once sang. I wish I could say the same for the other people who worked for you. Ten of your employees are no longer with us."

Ten! Michael could not bring himself to comprehend this terrible thing the doctor had said. Dear God, he thought, which ten of his beloved staff had died? Forming his lips for the word, Michael forced the air from his lungs into the word, "Who?"

Though the sound came out more like a long exhale than a word, Dr. Katz understood. "I can't tell you that, Michael," he said. "Rules. But General Prescott and some people in Washington have directed me to set up a Zoom call with you as soon as I think you're fit for it. It won't be today, that's for sure. You need more rest and nutrition first, and a few rounds with our excellent physical and occupational therapists before I throw you to the lions. The PT and OT will begin tomorrow. We'll see how you progress. I'll check back with you in the morning," he said, as he left the room.

Michael closed his eyes. Ten people. He knew all of his team members well. He hadn't been close friends with all of them—leaders couldn't allow that—but his core team had been with him for decades. He was close to all of them and their families. Dear God, he thought again. Please don't let me have caused this. He slipped back into sleep, his head swimming with images of the faces of all his people.

He slept fitfully throughout the day and night, only opening his eyes when the nurses made him do so. They asked him questions. They all but forced him to take food and drinks by mouth. Michael was sometimes belligerent, but understood he needed what they were doing. He couldn't remember much about anything after going to the Covid Clinic, but his memories prior to that were falling back into place.

He was determined to get out of his bed and out of the hospital. The nurses told him he'd lost twenty-five pounds while in the induced coma, and his usually powerful muscles had significantly atrophied. No wonder he felt weak. He was proud of maintaining a BMI—body mass index—of eight percent. Good for any athlete. Exceptional for a man in his mid-sixties. Now, it seemed, that was working against him. He needed to rebuild—and he was determined to do so quickly.

On the day after he began his OT and PT sessions, Michael was able to do pullups on the trapeze-like bar over his bed. Two days later, he was able to get out of bed on his own and walk—albeit slowly—around his room and down the hospital hallways. He could speak again, though his voice was still raspy. Feeling good about his progress, he asked Dr. Katz to arrange the Zoom call with Prescott and DC.

"Welcome back, Mike," John Prescott started. He was the only person who Michael allowed to call him "Mike". "I wish this call could only be to celebrate your survival. It can't. General Bob Atwood from the National Security Agency, David Hudson from the FBI, and Joan Henderson from ORR are also on the call," the general said. Each of the others raised their hands in acknowledgment. "I'll start by telling you who in your team did not make it."

He read off a list of ten names in a respectfully somber tone. Michael did his best to remain professionally aloof, but he could not keep from choking up. No person with a heart could have.

"John, your list did not include either Ron Rivera or Raúl Hernandez," Michael said. "Are they alright?"

"Rivera is good to go," Prescott replied. "No one is sure why. He was infected but sailed right through with only minor symptoms. I figure they'll be sucking his veins dry to run every test in the books on him. As for Hernandez, well, he's dead. What he wasn't, though, was truly on your team. Thanks to input from Rivera and your contractor John Pironti, federal investigators have uncovered a lot of dirt on the guy. I'll let our FBI participant fill you in, as much as he thinks he should. Before I turn things over to the others, let me say this: much has happened while you were in la-la land."

Prescott told Michael about the further uprisings around Holloman Air Force Base and in the neighboring town of Alamogordo. Many of the escaped refugees from the encampment on the air base had broken into homes there and taken them over. In some cases, they were welcomed in by the homeowners. The town of what was previously 32,000 residents was now closer to 100,000, counting the refugees. The entire town had become an armed encampment.

The UN Peacekeepers were doing constant Search and Seize patrols in an effort to recover as many of the escapees as possible. These patrols had led to gunfights between not only the UN troops and the refugees but also between the UN troops and American citizens of Alamogordo, who saw the Blue Hats as a threat to their own freedom.

The general told him that shortly after Michael had been admitted to the hospital, almost every citizen in New Mexico and northwest Texas had received texts and emails from a source identifying itself as the Department of Homeland Security, advising them to take up arms against the United Nations Peacekeepers. HAM radio operators in Alamogordo were sending out distress calls about being invaded and pleading for help. All of those calls and messages were fake, but 10,000 ranchers, farmers and wannabe militia members didn't know that. They showed up in droves, armed to the teeth.

"It's still a shitshow up there," Prescott said. "Over 5,000 killed, so far, and it's spreading. The UN has a "right to self-defense" in their charter, which says that while troops engaged in an operation may never take the initiative in the use of armed force, they are entitled to respond with armed force to an attack, including attempts to make them withdraw from positions which they occupy while acting under the authority of the General Assembly. Without any discussion with our DoD, they flew in 2,000 additional troops. The conspiracy theory blogs and podcasts are having a field day with that."

"Holy moly," Michael said. "Are we protesting that? Have we sent National Guard troops in there?"

"Just the opposite," General Prescott replied. "We don't have the troops to spare. The President and Secretary of Defense have welcomed the expansion of UN involvement. They are publicly blaming the uprising on 'right-wing extremists' and are calling for all Americans to lay down their arms and cooperate."

"Which brings us to the next issue," said FBI Special Agent David Hudson. "The text and email blast calling for help has all the earmarks of having come from your MassBlast system—or one similar to it. We can't prove it right now, but I don't believe in coincidences, do you? Since that virtual call to arms, messages like that have been sent to large groups of people all over the country, warning them about everything from poisoned vaccines to roaming bands of 'Covid Zombies' out to kill everyone. All the messages appear as being from some trusted government source. If there ever actually WAS confidence in a 'trusted government source,' that confidence is pretty much in the shitter, now. Don't worry, Michael, we aren't planning to take any legal actions against you or your company, even if our forensics teams tie this to your systems. The last thing we need is to have Fox News splash headlines about a fully vetted government computer system being involved. To make matters worse, Raúl Hernandez appears to have been the bad actor that opened your systems up for compromise. We discovered quite a bit when our teams cracked into his personal laptop. Strong indications of ties to North Korea. The son of a bitch had a fucking Top Secret clearance, for Christ's sake. You can imagine the witch hunts. That news would fire the country up if it became known. What we need from you is to surrender all your systems to us. We'll buy you out, of course. And you'll need to sign an airtight Nondisclosure Agreement."

Joan Henderson, from ORR, spoke next. "To coin a phrase, 'but wait, there's more'—and you probably won't like it," she said. "We've terminated your contracts with HHS and ORR, effective one week ago. As already stated by the general, a lot has happened while you were out of it. All refugee camps in the United States are now controlled by the United Nations—just like in the rest of the world. Many of us in Washington don't like it, and neither does most of the rest of the country. Not our call, though—it was done by Presidential Directive. Michael, we've already wired a final settlement payment to your account. We've paid you in full for the three years remaining on your contract, which is not a paltry sum of money. Again, you will be bound by NDA terms, just as with the FBI."

Michael said nothing. His mind was racing, trying to process all he'd been told and reconcile his own culpability in it. In fact, he had been thinking of an exit strategy for his business—this just wasn't the one he had in mind. He had much to consider, and it seemed he'd now have plenty of time on his hands to do just that. He would also have plenty of money to help ease the pain of his new status as a "retired tech exec".

His mental math told him that the ORR settlement would be north of $50 million, and a recent valuation of his business had come in at $10 million. Michael, a master negotiator, wasn't rolling over that quickly.

"You are putting me and a lot of other people out of work, friends. I'll need to take care of my remaining staff members—and the families of those who died. Worker's Comp Insurance isn't likely to help the families of those who didn't make it, even though they got the virus on the job. I've already been down that road with two other people last year. What they said then was something like 'when the contraction of COVID-19 is incidental to the workplace, such as when the worker contracts the condition from a fellow worker, a claim for exposure to and contraction of the disease will be denied.' And they did deny those claims. As much as I appreciate your generosity, for me to sign anything, I want the payments to be grossed up to negate the taxes or completely tax free. If you can agree to that, I'm ready to sign."

Henderson said, "We anticipated that, Michael. It's already been agreed to. The deposit in your account will reflect the gross-up."

"We're on board with that," chimed in Hudson. "We can discuss your price when you're back on your feet. Money isn't a concern, in this case. On another note, we would like to offer you a Personal Services Contract to work with FBI, NSA, and Cyber Command to dig deeper into Hernandez's activities. You knew him better than anyone. The compensation will be quite attractive, and you can pick your own team."

And just like that, Michael Conrad was a free agent. He already had ideas for his next chapter, and now he could afford to make them real. Already a well-off man, this windfall would be icing on the cake. His first thoughts were for his people, though. He would make sure that they would all be well-taken care of.

CHAPTER 7

GHOSTS IN THE MACHINE

AT HIS DESK inside the headquarters of the Basij Cyber Council, in Tehran, Bahram Mohadjer was smiling. His new trove of cyber treasure was a gift from his allies in Pyongyang, and his people were about to use it to launch new campaigns against The Great Satan—the United States of America. Considered a paramilitary force, Basij comprised mostly nonprofessionals, using volunteer hackers under IRGC—Iranian Revolutionary Guard Corps—supervision. These volunteers were sometimes referred to as "Cyber Commandos".

Bahram was proud of that designation. Thanks to injuries received on the battlefields in Iraq, he was no longer fit to lead his warriors into battle, but he was uniquely qualified to lead this group. He had graduated from the Massachusetts Institute of Technology, after all, with a master's in computer science. He understood technology—and he understood the decadent weaknesses of Americans. He hated Americans. His team at the Basij Cyber Council had been hitting them in their purses for years, with ransomware attacks and cyber scams, and now he had the tools to hit them even harder.

When serving directly under General Qassem Soleimani, leader of the elite Quds Force and Bahram's commander in the IRGC, he coordinated one of Iran's first major cyber-attacks back in 2012. His team of hackers knocked out over 30,000 computers of what was now the most valuable business in the world, the Saudi state oil company. His attack on Saudi Aramco prevented it from exporting its crude in one of the costliest hacks ever perpetrated.

His team of developers created a data-wiping malware known as "Shamoo'" that targeted the administrative computers of the company. He would have preferred to hit the industrial control systems used in oil production machinery; that would have been required a more elaborate and sophisticated attack, though, and his team was not then up to that task. Now, however, his proud Iranian hackers are increasingly focusing their attacks on critical infrastructure and the physical systems controlling things like oil refineries and electric utilities.

His team were, he grudgingly admitted, not as good as his Russian or North Korean allies when it came to the most sophisticated cyber-attacks, but they were experts at mining data to uncover "linkages" between seemingly arcane data and more high-value targets. This new trove of information held much promise, in Bahram's opinion.

It had been stolen from a system that supported several government agencies and contained a wealth of information within each record. By themselves, each record could bring as much as $1,000.00 on the Dark Web. He had almost one million records in this data cache; once his team had mined them, he would sell them to the highest bidder. But his mission was not to steal money from these individuals. It was to weave his way through the data to identify ways to compromise government systems and critical infrastructure systems. This data comprised accounts from employees of both. As the Americans would say, "easy pickin's!"

The coordinated focus of the cyber triumvirate of Russia, North Korea and Iran was to sew distrust and chaos within the rank-and-file population of their common enemy. Stealing money with a ransomware attack was not difficult but did little to accomplish the primary objectives. Such an attack did make for a news splash, if they were large enough, but quickly slipped from the minds of anyone not directly affected. In fact, ransomware attacks had become so commonplace that the general public had become desensitized to them.

Bahram's goals were to uncover more broad-reaching targets. Targets that every American would feel and be alarmed by. At the top of his list were elements of critical infrastructure, such as the power grid, cellphone networks, transportation, and fuel supplies. His partners in crime had developed ways to attack these targets and were constantly probing them for weaknesses—they just needed to uncover an opening. Bahram and his team members were going to find them.

"Greetings, Bahram," the Russian said in English, the language best understood by the three leaders of the cyber-triumvirate of Russia, North Korea and Iran. "Or should I say, *Hale shoma chetore?* My Farsi is terrible, I know, but I am trying to learn a few words!"

"*Zdravstvujtye, comrade!*" Bahram replied, using one of the few Russian phrases he knew well. "As you can tell, my skill in your language is no better—but thank you for trying! Let us stick with what we both speak well. How may I help you today?"

"It's been three weeks since we sent you the American database. How is your team progressing with it? You have good news, I hope?"

"We have made good headway, my friend," the Iranian replied. "To be honest, I've had to hold my team back from launching a few ransomware attacks—we've uncovered so many easy targets —to keep our focus on the bigger goal. That said, we have several targets that fit our primary mission. We will soon send a full report with our recommendations, but, for example, we have uncovered records on executives from major electric power companies, which operate significant portions of the infrastructure in each of the three main power grids in the USA.

We have home and work email and physical addresses, work and cellular telephone numbers, driver's license numbers, and their photographs. We have also uncovered the same types of data on both low and high-level American political and military figures. Interestingly, the data set also includes what appear to be janitorial staff. Tell me, what type of database would include such a diverse set of people?"

Sergei Alexandrovich laughed. "It seems crazy, no? The company our DPRK partners infiltrated enrollments and accounts for residents and visitors to camps for first responders, evacuation shelters and refugee camps all across America. As I understand it, power companies send large crews to restore electricity after a disaster such as hurricanes, tornadoes, or ice storms. Every one of those responders must be accounted for, so have their information added to this database. When their executives come to check on the progress, they, too, are enrolled. As for the politicians, they come to the evacuation shelters and refugee camps to 'demonstrate their concern' for the affected residents of those facilities. When they visit, they are also enrolled, as are every employee and visitor to these places, including members of the US military."

"*Ahmagh,*" Bahram said in his native tongue. "That means 'idiots.' You should add that to your Farsi vocabulary. Who would willingly give up such information? That would never happen in our countries!"

Again, Sergei chuckled. "Because our government leaders have demonstrated how such information can be used against a person! In fairness, the system we've compromised had passed every security requirement imposed upon them by the American government. If we had not infiltrated the company with one of our own agents, we would never have been able to steal this information. Once again, the Americans have underestimated our resourcefulness and our resolve. Now, we will make them pay for their arrogance."

CHAPTER 8

THE BREACH

FOUR WEEKS HAD passed since Michael had been released from the hospital. The first thing Michael had done upon getting home was to reach out to his friend and Chief Technology Officer, Ron Rivera. Ron had been with him in the company for over ten years, but a friend for even longer. He planned to make sure that Ron would be able to move into a comfortable retirement if that's what he chose to do. But Michael now had another thing on his mind. He knew that the federal government had deeper concerns about the risks posed by the breach of his systems.

They had been quite generous in their buyout offers and hadn't balked when Michael demanded tax accommodations. To his thinking, they would not do that unless there was more behind the scenes than they wanted exposed. The new contract offer was evidence of that, and he was excited by the offer. But he would need a smart guy like Rivera to pull it off.

During the weeks since getting back on his feet, Michael and Ron had made personal visits to the families of their teammates who had died, presenting them with substantial checks as a sign of their condolences. Michael wanted to make sure that each of the families would have a nest egg for their futures. The two men also leveraged all their connections within the government to dig into the background of Raúl Hernandez.

Both were frustrated and embarrassed that the man had been able to defeat not only the stringent background investigation processes, but their own well-honed "bullshit filters". What their backchannels told them was mind-boggling.

Raúl Hernandez had never tripped even one of the many alarms during the FBI Level II background investigation process. Nor had the top-secret security clearance investigators uncovered anything that caused them concerns. Every interview with his contacts was nothing short of stellar. His polygraph was passed with flying colors. He was, it seemed, the ideal patriot—and he was a minority. All good reasons to pass him through the system. Later investigations, though, had raised a few questions.

Raúl had been employed by two defense contractors at times when "certain secrets"—Michael's contacts wouldn't tell what these secrets were—made their way into North Korea. There had never been a direct connection between Raúl and those incidents, or any sound reason to suspect him until after the breach of ResourceOne's databases.

Because of the rapid onset of his Covid infection, Raúl had not had the opportunity to adequately cover his digital tracks, and they had been discovered by Michael's friend and security contractor, John Pironti. FBI forensics investigators verified Pironti's findings, leading to a search warrant for Raúl's apartment.

During the search, they discovered the man's private laptop, which was heavily encrypted, but once cracked by the FBI specialists, they found indisputable evidence of Raúl's involvement with the DPRK. None of this information had been publicly released, nor had the fact that Raúl had died. The laptop was now in the hands of the NSA and the US Cyber Command for further investigation and actions. Ron Rivera had been working closely with both agencies as they tried to determine just how much damage could be done by the compromised MassBlast systems. It appeared to be substantial.

"Good morning, Ron," Michael said. As per usual, Rivera had answered on the first ring. "Any input for me today?"

"Mornin', boss," Ron replied. "I do have a couple of things to discuss with you, but better to do that in person. The more I learn, the less I trust anything technological. And you know me—I didn't have much trust even prior to all this. I'll come over to your place right away."

Only twenty minutes passed before Michael's doorbell rang. Michael answered to find Rivera standing on the porch, his computer bag over his shoulder and two large—Starbucks insisted on calling them "Venti", which was actually Italian for "twenty"—cups of coffee in his hands.

"Thanks, amigo!" Michael said. "Nothing like a little Pike Place blend rocket fuel to fire the old synapses. I'm eager to hear what you've got."

As he fired up his Dell laptop, Ron said, "As you know, I was only sick with that shit for less than a week. Actually, I wasn't really sick at all, but I did test positive. The medics are still trying to figure that one out. Regardless, I was back in the saddle before the Federal shit hit the fan. That gave me some time to dig around a bit, based on what Pironti and I had uncovered regarding our boy, Hernandez. The fucking guy really did a number on the system, man. Best Pironti and I could tell, Raúl had, as most developers do, included a backdoor in his code. He never tried to hide that, but said he'd removed it prior to our first FISMA review. He actually must have done so, because the geeks from DC passed the system with flying colors. Thing is, he reopened the backdoor, just about a week before we had that first phony lockdown and fire drill. After snooping around, I found evidence that the entire databases of both MassBlast and our enrollment system had been cloned, using a standard feature of SQLServer 2016. That clone of the databases was then transferred to somewhere else in the cloud. That's where we lost track of things. When we first scanned for signs that our data had been tampered with or exfiltrated, the obvious answer was 'no.' Technically, that was correct. What we didn't initially know was that the cloned database HAD been exfiltrated. By now, you can be sure the Feds know all this, too."

"Ron, we had over one million records in those databases. You're telling me that some bad actor—most likely the DPRK RGB—now has a copy of all of them?" Michael was pissed. If Raúl had been in front of him, he'd have throat-punched the bastard. "Names, addresses—every kind of PII on the list. By all rights, we should be sitting across from a Congressional inquiry panel right now. But we aren't. That tells me the Feds are playing this low-key. Thoughts?"

"You read my mind," Rivera said. "They've sworn us to secrecy with those nondisclosure agreements and they haven't announced Raúl's death. That gives us an opportunity to set up a sting. We identify the most high-value, high-risk candidates in the database—then monitor the shit out of them. That window won't be open for long, though. You can be sure that Hernandez had some sort of reporting schedule to keep. Once we have some confidence, we can try to spoof Raúl's contacts into thinking all is well."

Ron turned to face Michael and said, "Boss, one more thing. I may have broken a law or two myself. As you know, I've always had the habit of saving an archival copy of our data onto a series of SSD drives that I kept on-site in a safe. Before I turned those over to the Feds, I made a copy of the most recent backup. I have it with me, right here. That's what I didn't want to say over the phone. I'll do whatever you want me to: destroy it, turn it in to the Feds as an 'oversight' on my part... or..."

"Or we can dig into it to see what we can see!" Michael said. "You're a fucking criminal, Rivera—and I love you for it! Now, get out of here. Meet me in a week at my place in New Hampshire. I have everything we need up there to dig into all this. I can't stomach the thought of being the cause of a situation that could turn into a genuine national shit show."

CHAPTER 9

THE COMPOUND

MICHAEL WASTED NO time in leaving El Paso. He returned home to his place in the White Mountains of New Hampshire—his own Fort Apache, as he called it. A one-hundred-acre secluded and gated compound, comprising a 4,000 square foot home, several special-purpose outbuildings, a fortified command bunker, a one-acre stocked, spring-fed pond, which also fed water to an underground cistern the size of an Olympic swimming pool, and a shooting range.

The entire compound was heated and cooled using geothermal systems, powered by solar, and had two thousand gallons of propane fueling two generators as a backup. He had both terrestrial and satellite-based internet connectivity and a HAM radio rig. The driveways and paths were heated for melting snow, and the gates each had pop-up hydraulic bollards inside and out, to protect against any attempt to ram a vehicle through them.

The computer room would rival most medium-sized businesses. Because of the nature of his work, the environment was designed to meet the stringent requirements of the Federal Information Systems Management Act—FISMA—and the DOD-required Cybersecurity Maturity Model Certification – CMMC (Level Three). The facility and systems had been successfully audited by the federal watchdogs. This was definitely not a "server in a bathroom" like a certain former Secretary of State had somehow managed to get away with.

The physical intrusion detection security systems, though, would stand up against any other facility, civilian or military. Aside from the expected array of cameras, Michael had installed "shaker" sensors on his fences to alert him if anyone tried to climb over them. He also had ground sensors in place to detect the vibrations caused by an intruder's footsteps, both inside and outside the twelve-foot-tall fences. These were part of an even more elaborate system from one of Michael's business partners, Senstar.

The crown jewel was Senstar's advanced RoboGuard Solution. An autonomous perimeter surveillance robot, RoboGuard, traveled on a monorail inside the fence, constantly patrolling the secured perimeter. It conducted regular inspections of the fence line and could also promptly respond to suspected intrusions. The system had two primary modes: routine patrol, in which the robot scans and searches for perimeter anomalies such as holes in the fence or suspicious objects and response mode, in which the robot acts as a first responder and rushes promptly to an intrusion alert.

Response mode included activating LED perimeter lighting, providing a live and recorded video feed to Michael's private security operations center, and a loudspeaker blasting a warning message. The robot was also equipped with a camera-aimed, five-round magazine-fed 12-gauge shotgun if that ever proved to be necessary. The entire system was powered by solar and had battery back-up.

With this state-of-the-art system in place, Michael always felt quite secure when at his mountain retreat. Still, he trusted people more than he trusted technology. The four men he employed as "groundsmen"—that's what he called them on his payroll ledger—were all former Army Rangers. These men were hand-picked and vetted and were dedicated to their mission: protect the compound and its inhabitants. They lived on the property and had full use of every amenity. Though they were on call 24/7, it was a great gig for a young soldier.

Ron Rivera arrived a week after Michael, as planned. The two men wasted no time in sorting through the massive database that Ron had clandestinely copied. The data was loaded onto a computer, which was kept isolated from the internet. Though Michael's cybersecurity posture was all but bulletproof, he wanted to ensure absolutely zero risk for this project.

"Let's start by separating the wheat from the chaff," Michael said. "First, identify records which might be of interest or value to a hacker. We can probably eliminate maintenance or housekeeping staff in this first round. Once that's done, we can circle back on those categories. They do still have almost invisible physical access to sensitive areas, so I don't want to rule them out just yet."

"Right on," Rivera said. "We're on the same page. I'm thinking we should look for government employees, military folks and people associated with anything deemed critical infrastructure, like power companies, pipelines, healthcare, airlines. Sound good?"

Michael said, "Yep. As you said—same page. Let's get busy."

Michael's company had been involved in responding to every sort of disaster and crisis for two decades. Their work had involved coordination with the executives of all the critical infrastructure elements that Rivera had called out, and more. The database included tens of thousands of senior-level people from each of them. Any one of them—or every one of them— was a potential risk for a nefarious actor on a mission. Michael and Ron had no illusions about their ability to stop any such attacks—they knew they couldn't—but felt their skills and experience might help identify a prioritized list of potential targets and the broader risks those targets posed. If the two cyber-sleuths could develop such a list, perhaps their government friends could alert potential targets and help them increase their awareness and security systems.

The men were three days into their project when Michael's power system alarm began sounding. During normal operations, his solar generation system delivered unused power back to the grid once his batteries were fully charged, for which he received renewable energy credits. If the "shore power" failed, his system alerted him, then disconnected from the grid and operated as a standalone solution. The alarm indicated such a failure.

"That's odd," Michael mused. "We just lost grid power. No bad weather—maybe some drunk took out a power pole somewhere. Let's check the news."

Ron Rivera said, "We lost terrestrial internet, too. We are now running over satellite. I'm hitting the news links now." A few seconds later, he let out a low, "Daaamn, man! Reports online say that the entire east coast is in a blackout!"

Both men began searching the internet for more information. They confirmed a massive blackout that covered the eastern seaboard from Maine to Virginia—the most densely populated portion of the US power grid element known as the Eastern Interconnect. No cause had yet been identified.

Michael's compound was specifically designed to be resilient in such a situation, as would be any home or business with a backup power source, like solar or fuel-powered generators. The percentage of such homes and businesses was small, though, with even fewer having the ability to be "off-grid" for extended periods of time. Michael's system would operate indefinitely. He had invested in such an elaborate, redundant set of systems because he'd been in situations of prolonged power and technology blackouts.

The first few days are like "an adventure". After four or five days, things get real. He had seen the social structure break down. He'd seen people who were dependent on medical systems like chemo pumps, dialysis machines and CPAP machines die. When frozen food thawed and spoiled, fresh water stopped flowing and waste couldn't be pumped, people became desperate—and sometimes violent.

Fights broke out at gas stations because fuel couldn't be pumped from the ground. Looting and robberies spread—sometimes out of desperation, sometimes out of greed. The resilient design of the compound ensured that Michael and his family didn't have to deal with all that.

There was a protocol established by Michael's family for situations like this. Even during a short power outage, his kids and a few others were to power on their satellite phones—gifts from Michael, because he was Michael freakin' Conrad, Master of Disasters! — and wait for further instructions. Michael would leverage his contacts and find out all he could about the cause and expected duration of the event.

If it was expected to last longer than three days or was a part of something bigger and more serious, the family were to make their way to the compound, using pre-planned non-interstate routes. All were to stay in contact, so one could help another, if needed. In the direst of cases, Michael, or one of his trusted team at the compound, would set out to find anyone who couldn't get there on their own. He had several pre-1975 vehicles on the compound, including a 1969 Nissan Patrol, two Ford F-100 four-wheel-drive pickups, and two fifteen-passenger Ford vans. With no electrical components required for the engines to run, these were the "survival rides" for that "just in case" moment.

Michael's gut told him that the "moment" had arrived.

CHAPTER 10

THE GENERAL POLITICAL BUREAU

SERGEI ALEXANDROVICH AND Won Lee Park sat next to each other at the long table in the presentation room of the General Political Bureau—the internal politburo of the Korean People's Army, now including leaders from Russia and Iran. Across from them sat ten of the most senior members in leadership of Russia and the DPRK, including Nikolai Platonovich, the President of the Russian Federation, Chairman of the State Council of the Russian Federation and Commander-in-Chief of the Armed Forces of the Russian Federation, Choe Ryong Hae, President of the Presidium of the Supreme People's Assembly of the Democratic People's Republic of Korea, and Kim Yo Jong, sister of terminally ill Kim Jong Un.

She was the heir-apparent of the Kim Dynasty and was actively engaged in the most important programs—especially those targeting America—but Choe Ryong Hae actually carried the most weight with the military leadership. Alexandrovich and Park had been summoned to give a detailed on their subversive activities toward the "American bastards". Speaking English would have been more than inappropriate in this setting, so an interpreter had been assigned to both the Russian and the Korean leaders. Park began the presentation.

"Lady and Gentlemen, I am pleased to report that our cyber triumvirate has made great strides! In fact," he continued, "we have an active cyber-attack underway at this very moment. We have darkened the entire east coast of our enemy, including the cities of Boston, New York, Philadelphia and Washington, DC—what they refer to as their 'Bos-Wash Corridor.' Millions are without power. We predict the outage to only last for a week, but it furthers our goal to shake the confidence of the Americans in their own government's abilities to keep them safe and secure. Like 'harassing fire' in a shooting war, it is meant to keep them off balance."

"Hullyunghan!" said President Hae. "This is excellent news! Please tell us how you accomplished this!"

"This was a collaborative effort," Sergei said. "Our friends in Tehran were instrumental in our efforts. Here, they helped us to infect thousands of small devices that make up what is known as IOT — the Internet of Things. These small systems are included in everything from major appliances to small ones. They allow a user to access their devices and appliances via the internet, for monitoring and remote control.

China, of course, is a major producer of the technical devices that the capitalist fools in America can't seem to live without. China has also been injecting these IOT devices with a cyber-virus for decades. Your enemy to the south is another major supplier of such appliances. Our Iranian friends, rather than try to hack into thousands of discrete devices, stole the source codes from China and from companies like Samsung and LG in South Korea!"

Park picked up the narrative. "Once we had the keys to these systems, we sent instructions to tens of thousands of large devices, such as televisions, refrigerators, and air conditioners, instructing them to shut down. Then, at a time we knew was normally a peak load period for their Eastern Power Grid, we caused these high-amperage devices to turn on simultaneously. The massive surge of demand caused their transformers to overload and shut down, which then had a wave-effect, causing even more of the grid to shut down. It was a brilliant plan and is working as we hoped."

"You have honored our glorious Republic!" exclaimed Kim Yo Jong. "Do you expect retaliation?"

"We do," Park continued, "but not immediately toward us. We have left a trail that leads directly back to our not-so-brotherly brother, China. By the time the American Cyber Forces figure out it was we who attacked, we will have executed more of our plans, driving them into chaos and anarchy! The Americans have been quite helpful in our efforts to infiltrate their country with our ground forces. Thanks to their porous borders, particularly their southern border, we have almost one million of our combined forces in place, awaiting our orders. When the bastards 'rescued' thousands of Afghanis and, most recently, the Eastern European refugees, we embedded thousands more of our Russian, Iranian and DPRK fighters and saboteurs within those groups. We are almost ready to strike them in ways that they will never recover from."

The group across from Sergei and Won Lee Park were more than pleased. Several shouted, "Strike now!" and "Don't wait!" and "Death to the American imperialists!"

"Patience, gentlemen," spoke Kim Yo Jong. "We are experts at playing the long game, are we not?" Turning back to Sergei and Park, she said, "Please, tell us more about your next plans."

"But won't our own infiltrators also be crippled by this power failure?" asked Nikolai Platonovich. "How have you planned for this?"

"We have, sir," answered Sergei. "Our sleeper cells had advance warning about—though not the precise timing of—the attack. They are also prepared for our next attacks, which will be more impactful and far-reaching. More importantly, they are poised to act once the time is right!"

"*Otlichnaya rabota!*" exclaimed President Platonovich. Sergei beamed. To hear "excellent work" from the president himself was something to be proud of!

CHAPTER 11

KICKOFF

MICHAEL'S SIGNAL APP alerted him to attend a secure WebEx meeting in thirty minutes on the topic of the blackout status. Leaders from North American Electric Reliability Corporation (NERC) and the Federal Energy Regulatory Commission (FERC) would be on the call, along with leaders of the Department of Homeland Security, FEMA, FBI and NSA. While he'd already received some back-channel information about what was happening, this would be the definitive discussion.

In 2006, FERC had mandated the establishment of an Electric Reliability Organization to develop and enforce compliance with mandatory reliability standards in the United States. This non-governmental, "self-regulatory organization" was created in recognition of the interconnected and international nature of the bulk power grid. NERC, a nonprofit corporation based in Atlanta, applied for and was granted the designation of the ERO by FERC.

In July of 2006. NERC also filed the first set of mandatory Reliability Standards with FERC, Cyber Security Standards—CIP-002-1 through CIP-009-1, "CIP" is the acronym for Critical Infrastructure Protection. All of this was done in response to the major Northeast blackout, which occurred in August 2003. That event lasted only for several hours but affected over forty-five million people in eight US States and over ten million people in Ontario, Canada.

The 2003 blackout's proximate cause was a software bug in the alarm system at the control room of FirstEnergy, which left operators unaware of the need to redistribute the power load after overloaded transmission lines drooped into a stand of trees and shorted out. What should have been a manageable local blackout cascaded into the collapse of much of the Northeast regional electricity distribution system. Very much like what was happening, right now, which was worrisome.

The leader of the teleconference was Susan Hardy, newly appointed Secretary of DHS. After the obligatory introductions, Susan asked NERC Chairman Dr. Steve Thompson to bring everyone up to speed on what was known about the current blackout.

"As you are all aware," Dr. Thompson began, "we have tens of millions of people affected by this outage. The entire Northeast Interconnect is down, with no firm estimate on the expected duration of the event. What we do know is, this was not caused by any physical issue, as was the blackout of '03. All indications are, this one is a cyber-attack. The failure did not emanate from a single source, but from thousands. Every grid operator and distribution company were hit with a massive demand spike, simultaneously, causing catastrophic failures of transformers and switches. Clearly, a coordinated action on the part of a bad actor—likely a Nation-State. Our investigation is ongoing."

Next to speak was Ed Sterrett, Deputy Director of the FBI. "For those who don't know him, let me say a word about the 'new guy' on this call. Michael Conrad is a contractor to several federal agencies, including mine and our partners over at NSA. We have him working a few angles that are better left unsaid. Regardless, Michael is a retired Ranger and a cybersecurity and IT expert. He and his right-hand guy, Ron Rivera, both served in the Army's Intelligence and Security Command, and both hold active top-secret security clearances. I've asked him to be a 'fly-on-the-wall' for this briefing. You'll all be seeing him again, I'm sure."

Michael gave an obligatory wave and smile, but kept his microphone muted. He would share his thoughts and opinions with appropriate parties once he'd digested all the information.

General Bob Atwood from the National Security Agency spoke next. "Dr. Thompson, are you saying this was direct cyber-attack on every power company on the Northeast grid, simultaneously? Seems unlikely to me. Please, explain your thoughts?"

"No," Dr. Thompson replied. "What we think happened is even worse. If it wasn't so bad for us, I'd give them a gold star for creativity. What seems to have occurred is, they hacked into thousands, maybe tens of thousands, of IOT-enabled appliances—that's Internet of Things for those unfamiliar with the term—forced them all to turn off, then forced them all to turn back on at the exact same time. The resulting massive surge blew up transformers from Maine to Virginia. Thousands of them."

"Holy shit!" Susan Hardy exclaimed. "How is that even possible? Are all those things the same? More importantly, how long will the grid be down?"

Thompson continued. "All IOT operating systems are not the same. But there are a handful that are most prevalent. They only needed to get into those to wreak the havoc they've managed to wreak. As for how long, well, that depends. Some areas will be back up before others—we have a priority based on needs. Fortunately, most hospitals and other critical facilities have generators. As long as they can get fuel, they'll be fine. Most residences don't have generators, however. Folks who depend on at-home medical devices are in trouble. Same goes for perishable foods—without refrigeration. Things will get bad after a few short days. Same with getting gas out of the underground tanks at gas stations. I'm sure our friends at FEMA are already working on plans."

"Right," chimed in FEMA Administrator Bobby Dunn, "we certainly are. POTUS rushed a Major Disaster Declaration, this morning, giving us the green-light to respond. We've already activated our Emergency Power contract holders, as have our partners at the US Army Corps of Engineers. As y'all know, we have large and small generators stored in our regional distribution centers, all maintained in a fully mission-ready status. We have started to deploy our resources and teams, to support our State partners. Under normal circumstances, systems would be deployed within forty-eight hours of getting the Notice to Proceed, but this new Covid variant is killing us—and I mean that quite literally. Affected States have begun to deploy what National Guard resources they have left. Covid and the recent full-scale military activation of their units have significantly degraded their response capabilities, unfortunately. What we are facing, in the terminology of my native South Carolina, is a genuine shitshow. We're doing the best we can, but we should all be expecting more than a few deaths, ranging from home generator fires and electrocutions to failure of chemo pumps, ventilators and other such devices."

"Susan Hardy said, "I'm still not hearing an expected duration from any of you. NERC, FEMA—let's fucking hear something!"

Dr. Thompson was the first to speak. "Ma'am, with all due respect, it will be a rolling recovery, like I said before. A full repair and restoration will probably take several weeks. Like everyone, the local power companies have been decimated by the BX6.5 bug. None are at full capacity. Like our friends at FEMA, we are also resource poor at the moment. In extreme cases—and I think this qualifies—we would ask our partners at FERC to formally request aid from the Department of Defense. DoD, however, have their own problems, right? Wars on two continents? Tends to strain an already weakened force—but you knew that, right? You can be sure that we are doing all we can, with what we have."

NSA Deputy Director Sarah Burton said, "Ladies and gentlemen, please. Let's stay focused on the issue at hand. 'Keep your head, when others are losing theirs,' and all that, remember? Madam Secretary, I'd suggest we let our folks at the forefront get busy. I would be pleased to work with you on establishing a battle rhythm for our Command Staff meetings. I can join you in the Emergency Operations Center, in twenty minutes. Does that work for you?"

Clearly flustered, but glad to see the situation defused, Secretary Hardy replied, "Yes, thank you. I apologize for being short with everyone, especially you, Dr. Thompson. I'll be including this group in a series of regular update calls. Dates and times will be sent shortly. Carry on—and good luck. Stay safe out there."

Michael came off mute. "Wait, what about the Alaskan, Quebec, Texas and Western Interconnections? What has NERC and FEARC done to prevent this from happening everywhere? Or at least preparing those folks for the worst?"

Silence.

Dr. Thompson spoke. "We have notified them of what we believe the cause was. All are reducing load, in preparation. Still, a comparable attack would still have significant impact on every one of them. Our teams are working on ways to detect new attacks, but because the IOT appliances are so numerous and so distributed, we don't see any way to stop it from happening again."

More silence.

"Turn off the internet," Michael said.

Everyone on the Hollywood Squares-looking WebEx screen had the same gape-mouthed look of shock.

"Wait," Burton said. "Did you just say, 'turn off the internet?' Really? Turn off the fucking internet? Pardon my French, but what the ever-loving fuck are you thinking?"

Not unexpected, Michael thought. "Thousands of IOT-enabled devices and appliances make up the body of this attack. We don't have the skills, time nor resources to kill every cell of that body. But as Muhammed Ali once said, 'Kill the head and the body will surely follow.' We need to cut off the head—the internet. No internet, no attack. Simple."

Silence.

Burton said, "He's right. As much of a political nightmare as this will definitely become, he's right. We'll need to brief the president and he will have to loop Congress in. Mr. Conrad, what would you suggest—in detail?"

"I'm not suggesting that we kill the entire internet, but we need to disable every non-critical account. Internet Service Providers know which accounts are residential, and which are other categories. I would recommend getting a directive from the FCC to every ISP in America, telling them to shut off every one of those household accounts. People will be pissed, but we can mitigate many of them being worse off—or dying."

After a few more minutes of chatter between the parties on the call, Secretary Hardy promised to keep everyone informed as to next steps from Washington, DC, then ended the WebEx. Michael was left with two thoughts. First, in his mind, the only two people on that call worth a shit were General Atwood, Director of NSA and Commander of Cyber Command, and FEMA Administrator Dunn.

Both had earned their roles through actual command-and-control experience in combat and during numerous disasters, since they were much younger men. All the rest were political appointees or businesspeople and obviously not dependable to keep their heads in the coming storm.

Second, he needed to call up his kids and alert them to come to the compound, immediately.

CHAPTER 12

PHASE TWO

S<small>ERGEI</small> A<small>LEXANDROVICH</small>, B<small>AHRAM</small> Mohadjer and Won
Lee Park were quite pleased with themselves. Their IOT attack had
worked just as they had hoped. Within forty-eight hours, they would
launch the attack on the Western Interconnection of the US power grid,
too. While they could have hit the entire grid at once, the goal was to
create fear along with the havoc.

Watching others suffer—and realizing that you could be next—was
terrifying. And this triumvirate was in the business of generating terror.
There would be a time for a mass attack, but it wasn't now, they thought.
Their chosen approach was like torture—many cuts are more effective
than one. If there was one trait that all three of their nations shared, after
all, it was their excellence in the dark arts of torture.

"Bahram, are we set for Phase 2?" Sergei asked?

"We are. Thanks to the trove of contacts in the database we stole
from the American contractor, we have everything ready to execute!"

In 2012, in response to Hurricane Sandy, Michael Conrad's
company had been contracted to build two 4,000-bed shelters in New
Jersey, to house utility workers from all around the country. One of
these shelters was built on the grounds of a defunct General Motors
plant, in Lindhurst. As a result, Conrad's company had many high-level
GM contacts in their database. Through a series of targeted phishing

attacks—known as "spearphishing" in the cyber world—Bahram's team of expert hackers were able to weave their way deep into the General Motors networks, ultimately getting to what they wanted—the command infrastructure for the GM OnStar System. Their attacks had allowed them to gain "super admin" access to the systems and then to install backdoor software. This allowed Bahram's team to seize control of the command systems, at their leisure.

By 2024, OnStar was installed in over one million GM vehicles, ostensibly for safety and security functions. But the in-vehicle safety and security systems also include the ability to remotely deactivate a car's ignition. This function can be—and often is—used in cases of car theft to prevent a stolen vehicle from being driven, or if law enforcement requests OnStar to shut down a car to apprehend a fleeing suspect. The OnStar system uses GPS to track the car's location so it can be deactivated, even if it is moving. Once deactivated, the car will lose power and come to a stop. The doors will also be locked, so the occupants can't get out.

And that was Phase 2: send a command to disable every OnStar-enabled vehicle in America.

Based on analysis by experts within the triumvirate, the impact would be massive, likely resulting in thousands of deaths along with the cascading chaos of shutting down a million moving vehicles, all across the United States. Gridlock, the likes of which could never have been imagined. But Phase 1 wasn't completed yet. Once the IOT hack was deployed across the entire North American power grid, the Phase Two attack would be even more impactful – and even more terrorizing.

First responders working to mitigate the impact of the massive power outage would be either themselves disabled by the OnStar attack or be caught up in the massive gridlock caused by all the vehicles that were disabled. A beautiful mess, thought Bahram, remembering a song from his days at MIT in Boston. Indeed, it shall be!

But Phase 3… that would be the coup de grace. That would be up to the other two partners, however, and set the stage for the fourth and final stage: Conquest.

Michael's first order of business after his WebEx was to text his family members on their satphones. He wanted them all inside his compound as quickly as they could get there. He knew that there was much more to what was going on than was being discussed on the call.

The hardest part was knowing that he'd have to tell three of his kids to hunker down and stay where they were. They all lived more than 1,000 miles away: the power outage would make finding fuel almost impossible, and their emergency reserve wouldn't be enough. He had made a good living – and stayed alive in more than a few dire situations – by listening to his intuition. Gut instinct had served him well. No reason to ignore it now. His message was short and clear: "Those of you who can get here on a single tank of gas, leave now. Take pre-arranged alternate routes. Arm yourselves. Reach out if problems. Communicate regularly. Jessica, Amanda and Andrea, hunker down and stay safe. I'll be in touch soon."

His second order of business was reaching out to Ron Rivera.

"This is getting weird, Ron. To make matters worse, there are only a couple of people out of the Fed that are worth a shit. We need to keep at our research and try to determine what we would do next if we were the bad guys. Think 'CARVER.'"

The CARVER matrix was developed by the United States Army Special Forces during the Vietnam War. The acronym stands for Criticality — a measure of public health and economic impacts of an attack; Accessibility – the ability to physically access and egress from target; Recuperability – the ability of a system or facility to recover from an attack; Vulnerability – the ease of accomplishing an attack; Effect – the amount of direct loss from an attack as measured by loss in production, or lives; and Recognizability – the ease of identifying high-value targets.

In other words, it is a systematic way to identify and rank specific targets so that attack – or defensive — resources can be efficiently used. The outcome of a CARVER analysis is a simple, uniform, and somewhat quantifiable means of selecting potential targets for possible interdiction. Michael had been using this approach successfully since his time as a Ranger. He knew it was statistically impossible to know every potential target that a bad actor may hit, but by thinking LIKE the bad actor, it was often possible to determine the most attractive of the possibilities.

Then you just needed to think like the bad guys – only even more bad than they think. For better or worse, Michael had a knack for conceiving devious plans. Ron Rivera was almost as nasty as Michael.

"Way ahead of you, boss," Ron replied. "I've combed our database for any records that have even a remote connection to any critical infrastructure-related entity. The good news is, I've found a lot of them. Bad news is…"

"Yeah, bad news is you've found a lot of them. Alright, amigo. I'll meet you in the secure conference room in ten. Let's see what we have, and which we should be getting after first."

Sitting across from each other in the well-appointed conference room, Ron and Michael toasted each other with freshly-brewed cups of Starbucks Pike Place blend. Ron had his laptop plugged in to the screen projector and had a list of critical infrastructure categories displayed on the large screen at the end of the conference room.

The list of sixteen were sectors whose assets, systems, and networks, whether physical or virtual, are considered so vital to the United States that their incapacitation or destruction would have a debilitating effect on national security, national economic security, national public health or safety, or any combination thereof. They were articulated in Barack Obama's Presidential Policy Directive 21 (PPD-21): Critical Infrastructure Security and Resilience and advances a national policy to strengthen and maintain secure, functioning, and resilient critical infrastructure.

The sectors include Chemical, Commercial Facilities, Communications, Critical Manufacturing, Dams, Defense Industrial Base, Emergency Services, Energy, Financial Services, Food and Agriculture, Government

Facilities, Healthcare and Public Health, Information Technology, Nuclear Reactors (including Materials and Waste), Transportation Systems, Water and Wastewater Systems. Leaders of each of these sectors had a duty to protect them from both physical and cyber-attacks. In fact, they had a presidential directive to do so. It was Michael's educated opinion, however, that most were doing a poor job, at least on the cyber side of things.

Due to the nature of their work, the ResourceOne database held records on senior-level people from most of the sectors identified in the list. The challenge for Michael and Ron was to pick the most likely candidates for being attacked by the bad guys. Clearly, the hackers had already exploited elements of the Communications sector, by using their own version of the ResourceOne MassBlast system to send bogus messages to members of the general public.

Sadly, they knew that particular genie was out of the bottle. The bad guys had the system, and that was that. Michael and Ron could not be sure whether the MassBlast database had any association with the attack on the Energy sector, but they had to assume that it did. The ResourceOne database held detailed contact information about hundreds of high-level energy sector executives.

It was certainly possible – if not probable – that one or more of these contacts had been compromised. Again, the men agreed, that was simply that – the clock can't be turned backwards. The question remained: what steps can be taken to mitigate further damage? Michael had offered the leaders from DC a suggestion, but he also knew it would be a heavy lift. Shutting down the internet for every "Average Joe" in America – during an election year – would not be an easy sell. It was, however, the only sure way to stop this particular attack from spreading. Such an order would take some serious balls, though, and there was a defined shortage of testicular fortitude inside the beltway.

Ron put his next slide on the screen. It was a CARVER analysis matrix, assigning a weight for each critical infrastructure-related record in the ResourceOne database, relative to each category of the CARVER model. The weights ranged from the lowest – one – to the highest – five – then totaled for each sector included in the matrix.

Based on the records stolen from their database, Ron had narrowed the analysis to nine sectors, including Chemical, Communications, Critical Manufacturing, Emergency Services, Energy, Government Facilities, Healthcare and Public Health, Information Technology, and Transportation Systems.

"Here's where it gets tricky. Every one of these sectors would have a significant impact if compromised. I've considered that, but I'm only concerned with projecting the risk of an attack via one of our database records. That's why even the most significant impact risk sectors are rated lower than a lesser impact sector might be. Make sense?"

"It does. We can't stop every bad thing, no question. I just don't want to have been the cause of the bad thing. I'm tracking on your approach, and I think it's a good one. Your matrix rates Energy, Transportation and Public Health as the top three most likely candidates for attack. What's your logic on those choices?"

"Our database has deep information on extremely well-placed individuals in each of those. Add to that the significance – both physical and psychological – of disrupting or disabling these systems and you have, in my humble opinion, prime candidates for an imminent shitstorm. Think about it. Kill the power, take out transportation networks, then create a public health crisis when the ability to respond to it is diminished. If that ain't a terrorist's wet dream, I don't know what is."

Ron was well-equipped to make such an observation. Michael had known the man since middle school. They had taken similar paths in serving their country – ROTC, Airborne School and Ranger School – but then their paths diverged. Michael had chosen to lead teams into combat. Ron had taken a more cerebral path, diving deep into information technology and finally as a senior officer in the Department of the Army Military Intelligence – Foreign Intelligence Analysis Directorate, aka DAMI-FIA' In that role, Ron had done more damage to terrorist organizations that even Michael's elite strike forces had. Michael hired him the day Ron retired from military service.

"Alright, Ron, get the contact info and your analysis off to our friends at Cyber Command. Maybe they can get ahead of whatever's coming next. I'll reach out directly to their Commandant, General Atwood. He's a solid operator and is probably the only one of that gaggle with both the juice and the chutzpah to do anything. Great job, amigo!"

CHAPTER 13

SLEEPER

LUCIOUS DAVID BALL – "LD" to all who knew him well – had always been a loner, but a "Good American". Born in what was then known as "The Ukraine", he was orphaned at a young age. At fourteen, he was adopted by the Ball's, an American couple from Alabama. He was raised with good American values. Did well in school and joined the Alabama National Guard while in college. That's where he learned to fly helicopters. What no one knew was that his adopted family were Soviet – later Russian — Sleeper Agents, recruited in the 1960s because of their political leanings. Once recruited, though, they were moved and given new identities, allowing them to not only blend in but to become pillars of their community. Both David and Sarah held low-level jobs at Redstone Arsenal, in Huntsville. The only task assigned to them by their Russian handlers was to adopt a teenager from Kiev in 1995.

By the time he was fourteen, LD had been well-indoctrinated. He'd spent seven years in a special orphanage, educated by die-hard Communists about the importance and glory of The Motherland. His training had been continued by the Balls, with the caution that no one must ever know their true loyalties. His time, they told him, would someday come. He would be called upon to let the world know who he was and what he stood for.

As he looked at the images on his computer screen, he knew that his moment would be coming soon. He felt fear and excitement – and pride. Whatever the mission is, he thought, I will fulfill it with honor, regardless of the cost.

LD was the first kid in his school to have a computer, back in the late 1990s. His pretty blue iMac was top of the line. He had remained a MAC user, because there was no better machine, in his opinion. And he had had an AOL account for email, such as it was back then. Only around forty percent of people in the US had an internet connection, so he was ahead of the curve, for sure. It was fun. It was cool. And it was an important tool.

He especially loved getting regular emails from his Uncle John – who wasn't really an uncle at all – who traveled the world photographing birds and animals. The emails came at random times and always contained one or two beautiful images along with run-of-the-mill greetings and chit chat about whatever part of the world "John" was in. But LD wasn't at all interested in the birds and animals. He was interested in the color palettes that made up the images. Because that's where the real message would lie once it came. Over the years, LD had, at the direction of his Uncle, moved from AOL to ProtonMail – a secure email service, based out of Switzerland.

Steganography had been used for centuries to hide coded messages within other messages. It is, in fact, an ancient art of covered or hidden writing. LD had been taught different methods of this art at a very early age and had always been fascinated by it. Now, instead of using simple word-based encoding methods, like taking the first or second letter of each word in a paragraph to represent the actual message, computers allowed more complex techniques.

With John's images, it was all about the size and makeup of the bits and bytes of the color schemes that made up the pictures. The technique became so much simpler with the advent of programs like File Juicer. Even more so when Apple incorporated the CAT function into Terminal Mode. Every picture John sent was different, but the palettes from which the colors were drawn were always the same.

Until today.

"Uncle John" – LD had no idea who the sender actually was – had sent a picture of three colorful Macaws. The first flag for LD was the number of birds. Three meant that there was more information contained within the coding or the image itself. When he decoded it, the hidden message was almost as cryptic: RED RAM AT NOON FRIDAY MORE TO FOLLOW. The message came in on Wednesday morning. LD felt excitement building inside him. After all these years, he knew he was being called to active duty. But what duty? Whatever, he was ready. Waiting another two days would be harder, though, than the last years had been.

After serving for three full contracts with the National Guard – twelve years – LD had taken his helicopter flying skills to the private sector. The Ball family had money, which he used to invest in starting an air services company. He shuttled people who could afford it between Huntsville and places like Nashville, Atlanta and the Redneck Riviera on the Gulf Coast. He also offered services for crop dusting, aerial seeding, and other such agricultural services.

His business had grown from a single Robinson R44 to a fleet of ten aircraft of various configurations. Along with himself, LD also employed five other pilots, all former military. Ball Air Services was based at the Huntsville Executive Airport, just north of town. They had a great reputation and business was always booming. Starting this business had been at the direction of his adoptive parents because they saw it as a means to their ultimate endgame. When they died, LD inherited enough money to continue expanding, always and anxiously waiting for the day that he could fulfill his parents' mission – and his own. With the new message from Uncle John, he figured that his waiting would soon be over.

The next forty-eight hours seemed to crawl by. Still no further word from Uncle John. LD went about his daily routine, just like every Wednesday and Thursday. Friday morning was no different. Until he saw the new email from Uncle John. It included an image of three Bald Eagles, sitting atop a barren tree on a mountainside. When LD deciphered the image, the message read: RED RAM SPARE WEAR

PPE MORE TO FOLLOW. LD was still unclear about the meaning but filed the message away in his mind. Like with every message he'd ever received from John, he immediately moved the email to a special folder within ProtonMail.

At 1150 hours, LD got a notification from his front gate security system. A vehicle had entered the area of the callbox, but no one had pressed the call button to request access to the gate. LD opened his video surveillance system portal to view the cameras. Parked in the entrance lane to his offices was a brand new, bright red RAM 1500 pickup truck. There was no driver. LD had one of his mechanics drive him to the gate, knowing full well that the keys would be inside the truck.

He told the man that it was a new company truck. LD was correct – the keys were in the ignition. He jumped in, drove the new pickup to one of the hangars used for servicing his private aircraft, and parked it there.

Once safely inside and sure he was alone, LD donned one of the HazMat suits used for spraying insecticides on the local cotton and bean crops. He went to the passenger side of the truck and removed the spare tire kit from beneath the seat. Then, to the back of the pickup, where he used the special crank to drop the spare tire from underneath the bed. He rolled the spare tire to the work area where his tire maintenance equipment was located, deflated the tire, and then carefully removed it from the rim. There was more than air inside the tire. There was a large plastic bag filled with a beige-colored powder.

CHAPTER 14

GAME ON

RON RIVERA WAS tenacious when it came to the investigative process. He was especially inspired to uncover all he could about how Raúl had managed to pull the wool over so many eyes and get past so many tripwires in the vetting process. He was also driven to determine the methods Raúl used to communicate with his handlers. Since no announcements had been made about the bastard's death, Ron wanted to attempt to game the gamers, as it were. To try to convince them that he was Raúl. What the fuck, he thought, what's there to lose?

Ron had pored over all of Raúl's company emails and files but found nothing of serious concern. On Raúl's personal laptop, though, he discovered a few interesting things. The first that caught Ron's attention were folders encrypted with BitLocker. Ron followed the usual steps in an attempt to find Raúl's BitLocker recovery key but wasn't successful. That meant that the guy had most likely saved it to a USB stick, memory card or other storage device. The FBI investigators had given Ron a box filled with various such devices – looking through all of them would take some time but there was no choice other than just getting on with it.

Another interesting discovery was the presence of OpenStego, a free steganography solution. The software was basic but had the capabilities of hiding data files inside an image or extracting the data from an image. At first Ron thought, "no fucking way any spy-type would use something this simple." Then he thought, "why the hell not?" It was so simple that it was counterintuitive. Subterfuge at its most simple is subterfuge at its best. As basic as the program was, it still required a password to use it. And the encryption was "mil-spec", utilizing AES-256 encoding. The AES solution had been around for quite a while but has never been cracked and is considered safe against "brute force" attacks. To Ron, that meant he was back to the problem of finding Raúl's cache of passwords.

Raúl also had a ProtonMail account. In Ron's experience, it was the most secure email platform available. Emails are end-to-end encrypted and one accessible with a security key. It was used by journalists, politicians – and ransomware thieves – across the globe. The servers are based in Switzerland meaning all data is protected by strict Swiss privacy laws and Swiss neutrality. The mailbox indicated that there were hundreds of email messages inside it, but, as with the first two discoveries, Ron would need the password.

Rivera went to the small kitchen down the hall from his workspace, poured himself a fresh cup of black coffee, then sat back to think about this mess he found himself in. He always found that stepping back a bit gave him a better perspective and allowed him to consider things from a big-picture frame of mind. What was he missing? What did he know about Raúl that could be helpful? He scribbled a few notes on a yellow pad. He was a fan of Mind Mapping as an approach to analyzing everything from software to warfighting. By the time he'd finished his coffee, Ron had a few new thought vectors to pursue.

Ron had traveled quite a bit with Raúl and was constantly amazed by two strange quirks the Cuban had. The guy carried a massively overstuffed backpack everywhere he went. Ron had seen Raúl's backpack piss off more than a few TSA Agents as they passed through security in airports from coast to coast. The other thing was Raúl's wallet. It, too, was bulging with every kind of credit card, receipt, seemingly random slips of paper – the thing was actually held together with five or six large rubber bands! Raúl answered no one's questions about why he carried those ridiculous items and always took the good-natured jokes in stride. Both the backpack and the wallet were in the crates the FBI had delivered to Michael's compound. Just maybe, Ron thought…

He went to the storage area where Raúl's things were. He grabbed the backpack and the wallet, then went to the large conference room and cleared off the mahogany table. Starting with the backpack, he began a systematic cataloging process of everything it contained. Books on system architecture. Several notebooks, filled with handwritten notes from meetings going back three years. Numerous ink pens and pencils, mostly from one tech vendor or another. Nothing to get Ron excited, other than hoping the passwords weren't hidden within the hundreds of scribbled pages of the notebooks. Then inside one of the interior pockets, he found something that did pique his interest: an IronKey thumb drive!

IronKey USB drives are fully encrypted and have brute force attack protection. Ten invalid passwords entered in succession and the drive crypto-erases itself. Any stored data is destroyed completely. The encryption was as strong as any of the other systems Ron was already frustrated by. Despite that, Ron was all but sure that this drive held the keys to the kingdom. There had been a lockbox in Raúl's apartment, containing almost one hundred flash drives. None of them IronKey drives. And this one was in the backpack that traveled everywhere with the guy. This is the key, Ron thought. I know it. But the bloody password!

Ron's next move was to pull up records from his company servers, showing every password that Raúl had ever used to access his work systems. People were creatures of habit. Maybe he had used certain patterns that could help Ron to figure things out. He found nothing useful. Raúl used different passwords, every time he was required by policy to change them.

Ron then began the cataloging process on the contents of Raúl's wallet. He had to shake his head in amazement. Receipts for everything from a two-dollar cup of coffee to three-hundred-dollar dinners. There was an overwhelming number of these paper slips, each neatly folded and tucked away. And then he found it. An American Express receipt from a tech vender named CDW for an IronKey Basic S1000 128 gig

USB flash drive! On the back of the receipt, a hand-written string of numbers, letters, and symbols.

The string of characters was written in what cyber-geeks called "Leetspeak' – letters replaced with various characters to disguise the actual words. Raúl had written *kU84L18Re072653* on the receipt. Ron used an online decoder to unscramble the string of characters – it translated to *CubaLibre022495* – the year the Cuban Revolution had begun.

"Bingo, motherfucker!" Ron shouted. "Not as smart as you thought!"

Michael stuck his head into the conference room. "What's all the noise, amigo? Sounds like you hit the lottery!"

"Close enough. I think I just outfoxed the fox that was in our henhouse!"

As he plugged the IronKey into the USB port on his computer, Ron explained the detective work he'd just completed. Once the IronKey login screen popped up on his monitor, Ron very carefully entered the combination of letters, numbers and characters from the receipt he'd found in Raúl's wallet: *kU84L18Re022495*. It didn't work. The screen flashed, then displayed a message that said, INCORRECT PASSWORD. YOU HAVE NINE ATTEPTS REMAINING.

"Fuck!" Ron shouted. "I was sure this was it!"

"Take a breath, Ron. What's the translation of the Leetspeak jumble?"

Ron turned to Michael and said, "Cuba Libre 022495. February 2nd, 1895. The date the Cuban War of Independence started. Looks like the bastard was smarter than I thought, after all.

Michael grinned. "That's the date the war started, but when did it end? That would be the actual 'Cuba Libre' date, right? Google it."

"Sonofabitch – you're right! Google says the Revolution ended on December 10th, 1898!"

Ron reentered the coded password, this time using *kU84L18Re121098*. It worked! The drive held folders labeled BitLocker, ProtonMail, and OpenStego. Inside the folders were passwords for each application.

"What's your plan?" Michael asked, sure that Rivera had a solid one in mind.

"Well, boss, first I'm going to decrypt the folders on his hard drive, then dig into the emails in ProtonMail. See if I can find any hints about how and with whom Hernandez was communicating. I'm pretty sure he wouldn't have OpenStego installed for no reason. I'll see what I can uncover in any image files I find. I have my work cut out for me."

"Are you planning to inform or engage the folks at Cyber Command? Might be a good idea to get them in the game as early as possible."

"Not just yet," Ron replied. "I want to understand all this better first. I'm hoping to uncover his methods, so that I can attempt to impersonate him. I don't want some young pup to jump the gun and blow this thing up."

"Copy that," Michael said. "But I do want to keep Attwood in the loop as soon as you think it makes sense. He's a solid operator and a great ally – don't want to alienate him. Keep me posted."

Ron began his work in his usual orderly fashion. Once into ProtonMail, he sorted the inbox messages by "sender" alphabetically and in descending order by the date the mail was received. He wanted to identify the most frequent senders and most recent messages. Raúl's most frequent emails came from "Tio Juan", and all the emails were in Spanish.

Ron was fluent in the language, having grown up speaking the language at home. Most of the messages were – at least on the surface – much like any expected from a caring Uncle. Many had image files attached to them. Of keen interest to Ron were the emails received within the most recent month. They complained about not hearing anything from Raúl in quite some time, asking if he was alright. The emails had stopped two weeks back.

Ron went to the "Sent" folder on the ProtonMail account and sorted the messages in the same way he'd done for the inbox. Raúl's last reply to Tio Juan had been the evening before he was hospitalized. It contained an image file. Sure that he was on to something important, Ron downloaded the image file and then started the OpenStego program, then loaded the image into it and instructed the program to decode the hidden message.

Within a few seconds, the Output Panel displayed: *Sospechas altas. Oscureciendo Más cuando es seguro.* Ron was doubly pleased. The encrypted image confirmed his hypothesis – and that was excellent news. More exciting, though, was the message itself. Raúl had put himself on ice because he knew he would be caught up in the investigation of the MassBlast breach.

I can use that, Rivera thought. But I need to measure twice and cut once. He knew he needed to read more of the emails, in order to be sure that he communicated in the same phrasing and syntax that Raúl used, and to embed the messages into images that were similar, as well. He spent the next few hours reading, analyzing, reviewing and planning. He created a timeline with every encrypted message exchange between Tio Juan and Raúl Hernandez. It read like a screenplay. Convinced that he was ready to take a stab at impersonating his deceptive former pal, he called Michael into the conference room.

"I'm as ready as I'm going to get, boss."

He showed the compilation of messages and their associated images to Michael, who slowly nodded in a sign of both approval and admiration.

"Great work, compadre," Michael finally said. "Tells a pretty nasty story, doesn't it? Looks like Raúl was up to his ass in this shit. If I'm reading this right – and I think I am – not only did he sell us out, he crafted the whole fucking thing from day one! And, he was knee deep in plenty of other crap, too, including the riots out at Holloman and the one at our own base. Obviously, a key player for the opposing team. If the motherfucker wasn't dead, I'd kill the bastard myself!"

"I feel you, amigo," Ron replied. "He was a key player, for sure. But now it's our turn on the field – and I don't do second place! We can't make things any worse, right? Put me in, coach!"

"Shoot your best shot, Rivera. Game fucking on!"

Ron had already teed up his message. It was embedded into a glorious image of sunrise over the Grand Canyon, which was in line with the other landscape-related images Raúl had used in the past. The message was short and simple, like many of Raúl's previous messages: *No descubierto y covid no me mató. Ya estoy de vuelta.*

They didn't out me and Covid didn't kill me. I'm back, read Michael. "Perfect!"

Ron hit the "Send" button.

CHAPTER 15

SHUTDOWN

THE MEETINGS IN Washington, DC had not been pleasant. When the leaders of the National Security Agency, Homeland Security, and the Federal Bureau of Investigation told the president and his National Security Council that the most effective way to avoid a repeat of the power grid attack was to shut down the internet for millions of people, the reactions were not pleasant. Decidedly unpleasant, in fact.

The president was first to speak. "Let me get this perfectly straight. You're telling me that now, coming into a national election, I need to order the shutdown of every residential internet account? Are you all fucking insane? Can we even do that?"

Sir..." General Atwood began. But he was immediately cut off by the National Security Advisor.

"General Atwood, do you realize what you're asking? The ramifications are huge. There will be riots – even more so than we are already experiencing. Maybe even an outright rebellion! Seriously, man..."

Atwood was having none of it. "With all due respect, sir, you need to sit back and shut the fuck up. I am a warrior, not a political appointee. I ALWAYS know what I'm asking and have ALWAYS considered the possible ramifications. As I was about to say, we don't think there's a realistic chance that we could shut down every residential internet account...at least not as quickly as we need to. There are over 8,000

ISPs – Internet Service Providers – in the USA. What we hope for is to get the largest ISPs to cooperate in the largest cities. Doing that will mitigate, to a significant degree, the effect of an attack such as we've just experienced. And remember, any internet connection serving businesses, government facilities and critical infrastructure will remain active. Browsers on cellphones will still work, as well. As to the question of 'can we do that?'…if you mean do you, as the president, have the unfettered authority to kill the internet, the answer is no, sir. That said, and as I'm sure your advisors will tell you, we've been working on a means to do so for a decade. Back in 2010, Senator Joe Lieberman introduced the 'Protecting Cyberspace as a National Asset Act'- called by the mainstream media and the conspiracy theorists 'The Kill Switch Bill,' which would have granted the president emergency powers over the Internet. As you can imagine, the ACLU and others dumped all over it. The proposal expired without a vote from either chamber of Congress."

"Then any such action to shut down the internet would require, literally, an act of Congress," the president said. "Am I correct in that?"

"Well, sir, yes and no," said Special Counselor to the president, Stan Richards. "You can issue an Executive Order for just about anything. As you know from experience, the Supreme Court can deem it unconstitutional, thus negating it, but that takes time. Bottom line is, you can do whatever you want – for a while."

FBI Deputy Director Ed Sterrett said, "Sir, the FBI has been working with the large comms companies on this since before my time here. Technically, it can be done. Politically, and to be blunt, it would be a shit storm. Especially now, while this new Covid variant is rampant. We have kids learning from home, telemedicine for homebound patients, all that. I agree with General Atwood that shutting down the net would mitigate an attack on the power grid, but it's the unintended consequences that I'm worried about. Frankly, the idea of flipping an internet kill switch scares the bejesus out of me."

"As the Director of the National Security Agency and Commander of Cyber Command," Atwood continued, "I'm giving you all the hard-ass facts of life. We have two choices, in my educated and considered opinion: Shut down the internet or suffer a much broader – probably nation-wide – attack on our power grid. If you choose the latter, I will tender my resignation forthwith. Make your choice. We are out of time!"

The President of the United States slowly rose from his seat at the head of the Situation Room conference table. His tenure had been a difficult one, to say the least. Covid shutdowns, inflation, fuel shortages – topped off with deploying troops into harm's way on two continents while the United Nations was deploying their troops inside of the US. Now, this.

"Gentlemen, stand down. General Atwood, if I didn't trust and value your opinions, I would not have nominated you for the roles you have performed so well. Stan, prepare the Executive Order. This meeting is over. May God help us all."

Atwood's next call was to the Chair of the Federal Communications Commission. He had already briefed her on the situation – now it was to order the action. She was incredulous, but knew that it was necessary. Chairperson DeAngelis had already written the preliminary notification, ready to be sent if and when she was directed to act. The initial email would be followed with certified mail letters and direct phone calls to the presidents of the largest common carriers and cable-based internet service providers. DeAngelis could feel her heart racing. The defecation is most certainly about to make contact with the rotary oscillator, she thought.

She was right.

Within minutes of getting the call from General Atwood, a copy of the newly-drafted Executive Order was in her inbox. She attached a copy to the email that she'd previously drafted and hit the Send button. Moment later, the switchboard at the FCC was on fire. Chairperson DeAngelis did not accept any of the inbound calls. Instead, she fired off another email, which included an invitation to a mass WebEx, to be held in fifteen minutes. Not that any of the ISPs had a choice in the decision: the presidential directive mandated they comply immediately. DeAngelis knew the carriers would scream to the high heavens about this action. She also knew that the press would not be far behind.

She was right again, on both counts.

The FCC switchboard received calls from all the major news

organizations, asking for comments and confirmation. As with the ISPs, DeAngelis declined to speak with any of them. This is a problem for the spin doctors at 1600 Pennsylvania Avenue, she thought.

Saying anything to the mainstream media is a bad idea. Saying nothing, a worse one. No government agency head relishes being the subject matter of BREAKING NEWS! Yet here she was. Her face and the words "FCC Mum About Internet Shutdown" were on the news websites and cable news shows within an hour. Twitter virtually exploded with posts and comments. None were positive. Not that Twitter or the websites would be an issue for much longer…

Michael's cellphone rang, displaying a 202 Area Code number. Washington, DC.

"Conrad, Atwood here," the caller said. "By now, I'm sure you've seen the news. As amazing as it seems, they bought off on your idea. The majority of residential internet services will be shut down within the hour. No way to get them all, but we believe it will be enough to reduce any impact from another IOT-based grid attack. You gonna be good?"

"We're good. All commercial wired interconnections at my place, backed by commercial grade satcom. My Fed contracts give me an advantage, too. I'm sure you're about to have your hands full with the rest of America, though. Streets are bound to fill up, pretty damn soon."

"Yessir," Atwood replied. "It won't be pretty. Our intel is that ANTIFA is already calling for outright rebellion. Thanks to our active duty troops and most available National Guard units being deployed, and many of those that aren't deployed down with BX6.5, we will have a hard time responding to whatever they throw at us. We've seen what happened in Egypt, China and, to a lesser degree, Turkey. The blowback will be huge. No one in DC thinks the Executive Order will stand for long. SCOTUS doesn't take well to violations of the First Amendment – which this clearly is. We just hope that it will buy the power companies enough time to harden their most sensitive infrastructure. The clock is definitely ticking."

"Copy that, sir. This also throws us a new twist in our plan to spoof the bad guys with Raúl's account." Michael had already spoken with General Atwood. He had explained the progress Ron had made and the go-forward plan to try infiltrating the attackers. "Raúl had been communicating exclusively via his personal accounts. Except for allowing access to our corporate systems, we haven't seen evidence of any direct connections to any suspicious servers. Everything has been through a secure email platform. We will have to devise a scheme that will make it appear that his communications were screwed along with the rest of the country. I have some thoughts, but need to run them by Rivera before I'm comfortable discussing further. With your permission, I'll get busy with that right now. Conrad, out."

"Take care of business, Colonel Conrad. As I said, we won't have much time. If what you told me about Raúl Hernandez's depth of involvement with these asshats, you're our best hope in getting a handle on what else they're planning. And when. Atwood, out."

Ron Rivera shouted from the next room. "The fucking internet is down, boss, pretty much coast to coast. We're good, obviously, but the news outlets are reporting an internet usage drop of over seventy percent in the last thirty minutes! Most of those people are sure to bombard the cell networks with heavy demand. I can tell you that the cellular providers don't have the capacity for all that extra traffic. Anyone accessing the net through their cellphones are going to experience glacial speeds – if they can get a connection at all. Shit's getting real, amigo."

CHAPTER 16

UNINTENDED CONSEQUENCES

"THIS IS UNBELIEVABLE!" Sergei exclaimed over the secure phone line connecting him with his two partners. "The Americans are shutting down their internet! We need to execute Phase Two immediately!"

The news of the unprecedented action taken by the American government had quickly gone global. It was being both praised for its necessity and lambasted for its brashness. The triumvirate of Russia, Iran and North Korea, however, viewed the move as a threat to their larger plans. Not all their plans depended on accessing the American internet, but certain critical plans certainly did. Like Phase Two.

"Phase Two involved a broader strike on the American power grid, using the same IOT-based attack that had proven successful in the Northeast of their country. That attack had been a trial run. More importantly, it had caused the Americans to deploy power company resources from many other states, leaving them vulnerable. Phase Two also included a physical attack on large transformers and switching stations, in an around the cities affected by the IOT attacks.

There had been several trial runs of such attacks perpetrated by what the Americans thought were "lone wolf" operators, simply creating mischief. What the triumvirate had learned was just how easily such attacks could be carried out, especially if there was already a major event underway.

"We need to execute Phase Two right now, including the physical attacks," Barham said. "Can you activate the ground forces without internet?"

"We can," replied Won Lee Park. "The news reports say that cellular internet is not affected. Our teams use WhatsApp and Signal as backup to the ProtonMail and image file methods. Not our preferred method of communicating, but we are left with no recourse. Regardless, I agree. We need to execute Phase Two immediately. Maybe we aren't too late for the IOT attack, at least in some areas. Bahram, have your team execute that, straight away. I will send orders to attack the physical systems that we've designated. Our shooters are in place and know their targets. Those attacks can happen tonight."

"What about Phase Three? I think we should hit those *ʋbʼlʌdʋk* hard and fast!" Realizing that the Russian word he'd used would not translate well to either Farsi or Korean, he continued, "I'm sorry. That word describes one who has sex with his own mother."

Bahram laughed. "You mean 'motherfucker!' One of the side benefits of attending university in America is that you learn all the good curses!" More soberly, he said, "We are on it, my friends. And I agree, it's time to hit them from multiple vectors."

"Patience, my friends," Park said. "We North Koreans are experts at playing the long game. Timing for Phase Three must be perfect to be most effective. It will lead directly to the final phase. We aren't quite ready for that yet."

Robert Watson was in line at Tractor Supply Company when his phone chirped with a notification from WhatsApp. He hadn't been able to get online all day, even using his cellphone. The news about the government killing the internet was everywhere, but they had said the cell networks wouldn't be affected. Of course, that meant that everyone with a cellphone was trying to get online at the same time. The networks were saturated, making connections slow, if a connection could even be had.

He looked at his message. It read: "Do it – tonight." He knew what that meant. He could feel his heart speed up. The hardest part of his role as a dark agent was the waiting – he had never been a patient man. He had also never even met the people who had been paying him for the past three years. He had been contacted though an online forum he was a part of, specifically for folks of his own political leanings – so far to the right that he made Atilla the Hun look like a liberal fag.

His last job had been to deliver a load of MREs to a protest rally outside the fence at Holloman Air Force Base, where the UN Blue Hats had started what he and his compatriots thought of as an invasion. Along with the cases of MREs had been one special case. A box filled with twenty-five pounds of Tannerite. He then drove his pickup to a highway overpass and fired a single round from his AR-15 chambered for .308 Blackout. The explosion had rocked his truck, even from a half-mile away. That mission had resulted in not only a great sense of satisfaction, but a substantial increase in the balance of his Coinbase Bitcoin account.

Tonight, he would once again get to use his weapon to bring down some shit on the current government of the United States and their UN allies. Robert wasn't in this game for the money, though he knew this gig would pay even more than the last mission had. Robert had an axe to grind. He was a proud American who had served his country with honor. He enlisted in the US Navy right after earning his bachelor's degree. He wanted to be a warrior – and that's what he became. The best of the best. A Frogman. A United States Navy SEAL. He fought, bled and killed to uphold his oath: *to defend the Constitution and laws of the United States of America against all enemies, foreign and domestic; and bear true faith and allegiance to the same.*

Then the Navy and the assholes in the Pentagon fucked him over because he refused to take their shot of poison. He, along with a couple of thousand other soldiers, were punished or discharged over a fucking choice about their own bodies. Faced with the disgrace of losing his slot on SEAL Team Six, Robert opted to resign. That pissed him off. A pissed off SEAL makes for a bad enemy. The US government — the "domestic enemy" – was about to figure that out.

Robert knew his target. He'd scoped it out many times. And he knew his mission: to blow the fuck out of a large power transformer on the outskirts of Dallas. He was fired up about this one – and he was ready to rock!

Shortly after midnight, he headed out. When he got to the substation, Robert first cut the fiber-optic communications lines, shutting off service to nearby neighborhoods. Then, he fired more than 100 rounds of .308 Blackout ammunition into the radiators of 17 electricity transformers. Based on the instructions from the folks who set him up for this mission, his attack would cause thousands of gallons of oil to leak, causing the transformer electronics to overheat and shut down.

From what he could tell, the results were exactly what was expected. As he drove away from the scene, all he could see was darkness, punctuated by random pools of light, obviously from homes and businesses with emergency generators. Scary cool, Robert thought. Scary fucking cool.

What Robert didn't know was that there were over one hundred identical attacks going on at the same time. He also didn't know that he was playing a role in "Phase Two" of the Triumvirate's plot to take down the critical infrastructure of the United States.

"Bad news," Barham said to his triumvirate partners. "By shutting down their residential internet services, the American bastards have effectively stopped our IOT attack. We could contact many devices, but not enough to cause the impact we wanted. How goes the physical attack?"

"We are getting reports of great success with that!" exclaimed Park. "We're seeing massive power blackouts in over one hundred locations. Tens, maybe hundreds of thousands of homes and business are dark. Certainly, this would have been of better effect if the rest of the plan had worked, but our goals are being accomplished. The Americans are struggling with resources, thanks to our first attack and the impact of Covid. Our plans to sew discontent and distrust are working. Our agents report mass protests and violent actions in the larger cities. Our leadership is pleased!"

Sergei spoke, "The whole series of events is also impacting our own resources, however. With the internet down and now major power outages, communicating with our ground forces in the US is a problem. Our cell leaders have satphones but most of their key people don't. Our own actions are having unintended consequences – for ourselves."

"One more thing to discuss," said Park. "We've had contact from Raúl Hernandez. I was sure we had lost him. He says that he was sick with Covid and had also been under scrutiny from the American FBI. He goes on to say that he's in the clear and ready to reengage."

"Can we trust that it's him?" Sergei asked. "Not someone impersonating him?"

"Our team has high confidence that it's him, based on the messages and the encrypted images he sent. But we have another test to implement, just to be sure. We are sending that out today. If it is Raúl, we are in luck. He knows so much and is a key resource for us inside the American quagmire. I will report what we discover. For now, signing off." With that, Park ended the encrypted video call.

As confident as he'd tried to sound on the call, Won Lee Park — the north Korean spy master – was still nervous. He tapped his pen against the table. He had to be absolutely sure that it was Raúl sending the messages. The messages had been appropriately cryptic, laden with all the proper code. Still, Park had to be sure that Raúl had not been compromised or was being impersonated. He decided to have his team send a WhatsApp message to Raúl, asking him to prove himself by telling something that only he would know.

Park's team sent the message in English: *What was your first mission?*

CHAPTER 17

ESCORT MISSION

WHEN MICHAEL RETURNED to the conference room – now dubbed the War Room – at 0600, Ron Rivera was already focused on his computer monitor. He looked up.

"Shit's getting weird, boss. We have reports of over 100 physical attacks on power switching stations last night. Most of the power in the country is down. First reports all indicate the attackers used high-powered rifles. Also, there was another attempted IOT attack. It had some impact, but thanks to your suggestion of shutting down the residential net, no real damage was done. If nothing else, this is pretty solid proof of an organized attack on our infrastructure, wouldn't you say?"

"Well, Captain Obvious, I most definitely would say that. Question is, which of our favorite adversaries should we hit back? All indications are Iran, but to no one's surprise, they deny it. They're pointing their finger at China. It could be anyone from a domestic group to Russia – who are now operating out of Pyongyang – to North Korea themselves. Too many suspects are as bad as no suspects at all. My money, though, is on North Korea."

"But wait, there's more!" Rivera said, mimicking the old TV pitchman, Billy Mays. "Our Raúl WhatsApp account got a message from "Tio Juan". I assume they're using WhatsApp because of the internet outage. He is asking Raúl to tell him what his first mission was. We know from the FBI info that the first they actually suspected was stealing from Raytheon, but it wasn't proven. It's the best we have, though. I recommend we go with it. We have a fifty-fifty chance of being right, statistically speaking."

"Old buddy, there's an old saying that anytime you have a fifty-fifty chance, there's a ninety percent probability of picking the wrong answer first. But, as you said, it's all we have. If it works, we're in. If not…"

Ron typed the reply: 'Raytheon. Standing by.'

Michael placed a satphone call to General Atwood, telling him of the message to Raúl and how they handled it. He also made a special request of the General.

"Sir, as one old Ranger to another, I need a fairly large favor. I need two airlifts to get my kids up here to my compound. One from Scott Air Force Base in Illinois and one from Pope Field at Bragg. We both know the shit is getting real out there. Can you help?"

"Michael, as you are well aware, in the Ranger Creed we promise that we will never leave a fallen comrade to fall into the hands of the enemy. As far as I'm concerned, that Creed lives forever — and it applies to our families, too. I'll call in a few chits, then get back to you with a schedule. I'd suggest you have them prepared to mobilize as soon as this afternoon."

"Much appreciated, Sir. If you can get them to Pease ARB, down in Portsmouth, that would be outstanding. I'll take it from there. Sadly, none of them are airborne qualified, or I'd just ask you to drop them off at about 1200 feet above my house."

General Atwood laughed. "I figured you'd have pushed them out of perfectly good aircraft at an early age! You disappoint me, Ranger Mike! Stand by for further input. And let me know how your Raúl gambit plays out. That could be a real break for us!"

"We're in!" Ron shouted. "They bought it. The responded with "Welcome back". How do you want to proceed, boss?"

"We need to get them back to using email. I want a trail and we can't get that from WhatsApp. Send the next message using the steganography thing. Tell them that you are working out of this location. Raúl was here many times and surely must have told them about it. Tell them you have full internet access. They've taken the bait. Now let's set the fucking hook!"

Ron composed the message to "Tio Juan" in Spanish, as was normal for him. He wrote:

Estamos trabajando en el complejo seguro de nuestros jefes en las montañas de New Hampshire. Internet comercial completo sugerimos. Que volvamos a este método de comunicación.

Once Michael approved the message, Ron used the OpenStego software to encrypt it into an image of a snow-capped Mt. Washington, accessed Raúl's ProtonMail account, then hit the send button.

Then they waited.

Michael's iridium satphone rang. He had installed indoor satphone amps and repeaters throughout the compound to ensure he could take and make calls while inside. It was General Atwood.

"Ranger Mike, your mission has been approved. We can transport from both locations at 0600 tomorrow, local time. That's a no bullshit time, and there won't be another opportunity. Flight time will be one hour and fifty minutes from wheels up. The two locations are approximately equidistant. Because of the time zone difference, the flight from Pope Field will arrive an hour earlier than the one from Illinois. You can pick everyone up by 0930, Eastern Time. You good?"

"We are good to go, sir. Thank you very much. You can call in this chit at any time – I'm there for you."

Atwood laughed. "Oh, don't think that won't happen, buddy. I have you on speed dial! Atwood, out."

Michael immediately called his daughters in South Carolina and Illinois, relaying the plan. Both balked at first, because of who they were – dedicated professionals providing needed services. They both felt obligated to support their communities and their employers. Michael admired them for that, but finally convinced them that this was a time when the family takes precedent over anything else. They both agreed to get their immediate families to the airfields in time for the flights.

Michael next pulled his Kenwood ProTalk PKT-23 radio from its belt holster. He needed to get two of his "groundsmen" prepped to roll out at 0500 tomorrow.

"Eagle Two, Eagle Three, Eagle One, please report to the main house ASAP, over."

"Eagle Two, copy. Wilco."

"Eagle Three, copy. Wilco."

"Eagle One, out."

Eagle Two was the callsign for Ranger Jack Sims, a man who Michael trusted as much as he trusted anyone. He had worked at the compound for over ten years, since leaving the Army.

Jack had always known that he wanted to serve his country. He joined the US Army straight out of high school and worked his way up to become an Army Ranger – the top of the crop. He was dedicated to his job, always pushing himself to be the best he could be.

After twelve years of service, Jack needed a change. He had done five combat tours, and it was now time to take a step back from the front lines. He decided to leave the army and start a new career in the private security sector.

As with most vets returning to "The World", the transition was challenging. Jack missed the camaraderie of his fellow soldiers and the sense of purpose that came with serving his country. He soon realized, however, that his skills were just as valuable in the private sector. More so, from a financial perspective.

When Jack received a call from an old army buddy, his world changed. His buddy told him about Michael and offered to set up a meeting. The rest, as they say, was history.

Michael's work was all about supporting the nation in ways that only a private contractor could. Not only did that all fit him to a tee, Jack rediscovered the sense of purpose that he had been missing since leaving the army. He was dedicated to his new work and his loyalty to Michael Conrad was deep and strong. He'd often said, "I'd run through a flaming wall for that man!" and he meant it.

Eagle Three was the callsign for Darius Bending. Dar's story was similar to Jack's. Fact was hundreds of Army Rangers had stories similar to Jack's. That's just the profile. In Dar's case, his time in service was cut short by an IED. He and three Ranger brothers were hit by the same bomb. He fared better than the others. They both died. Dar lost his left eye and sustained some serious structural damage. He was told that, while he could remain in the Army, his Ranger days were over. For Dar, being a Ranger WAS the Army. He opted for a medical discharge.

During out-processing, one of the counselors talked to him about opportunities in the private sector and gave him a list of contact names. After doing his best to settle in to life as a civilian, Dar knew he needed more. Like Jack, he felt he was missing a sense of purpose. He started down the list given to him by the counselor. Triple Canopy, GuardaWorld, Acadami – the leaders in the industry. None of them tripped his trigger.

Then, he saw a posting on a chatroom for former Rangers, about a gig in the White Mountains of New Hampshire. That turned out to be the job he now held with Michael Conrad. Dar felt he'd found a real home with a group of like-minded people. A new Band of Brothers, all of whom were Ranger-qualified. And the pay and bennies didn't suck, either.

Both men were prepared to execute any mission their boss assigned to them, without questions, concerns, or hesitation.

"Gentlemen, take a seat," Michael said, when the two men walked into the conference room. "I have an important mission for you, outside the wire. I don't expect it to be dangerous, but things are getting weird out there. As always, you should be prepared for the worst. I need you to drive the two fifteen-passenger vans down to Pease to pick up my kids and their families. I'd expect the thirty-gallon tanks will be enough fuel for the round trip, but you should each bring two five-gallon Jerry cans, just to be safe. You will leave here at 0500 tomorrow. One group will arrive at 0800 and the second at 0900. You'll both wait for the second flight – so don't separate. Bring them directly back here. Any questions?

"No, sir!" the two Rangers said in unison.

Ron Rivera looked up from his computer screen and held up his hand.

"New news, guys. I'm seeing reports of random car jackings and roadblocks near Portsmouth. As Michael said, things are getting weird out there. Fuel has become a valuable commodity and people are getting killed over it. Keep your heads on a swivel."

"Roger that," said Jack.

"Copy all," replied Dar. "We're out of here."

Michael considered sending all four of his Ranger "groundsmen" on the mission, but thought better of it. He wasn't prepared to leave the compound unguarded, especially since they had told Tio Juan that Raúl was operating from there.

"Strap up, boys. And bring a couple of extra toys for the passengers. See you when you return."

The two Rangers were always up by 0400. Leaving at 0500 was no big deal. They decided to take Route 16 South all the way to Route 125, where they would exit and take back roads the rest of the way to Pease Air Reserve Base. They wanted to avoid the toll booths at Rochester and Dover and didn't want to go onto I-95 South. Too close to Portsmouth and too many choke points, which meant they would be perfect for ambush locations.

Both men brought M-4 carbines with 60-round double stack magazines, plus four spare magazines each. Each also carried Sig Sauer P-226 pistols with extra mags. In each van were two more sets of the same gear as Michael had instructed. In the hands of these men, the cache of weapons and ammo would be enough to put down a moderate-sized insurgency.

Along with the weapons, both men carried iridium 9575 Extreme PTT sat phones. Those devices included location tracking and push-to-talk functionality. Michael and Ron could check on them anytime they chose to, and they could contact each other or their base with a single touch of a button.

The two vans rolled out of the compound right on the 0500 mark, quickly establishing their "open column" convoy spacing of 300 feet apart. They would maintain the legal speed limits, as posted, unless the shit hit the fan. Should that occur, they would adopt an "infiltration" formation and do whatever the situation dictated. This was not either man's first rodeo.

The two-hour drive to Pease was uneventful, other than the curious and sometimes glaring stares from groups gathered in the few small towns the Rangers had to pass through. There was no traffic other than a couple of police cars and a few motorbikes. Not one gas station was open, but every one of them had non-working cars spilling out of their lots.

Jack pressed the PTT button on his phone.

"This is some eerie shit," he said.

"Fuckin' A, brother," Dar replied. "Some of those folks we passed in Ossipee looked at us like they'd take us out if they had half a chance."

"Boys," Michael chimed in, "That ain't happening. You get the mission accomplished and take no shit from anyone. Your asses are covered. Be advised, though: try not to kill anyone who hasn't tried to kill you first."

"Copy that, sir," Jack said. "We will report as things progress."

The two vans arrived at Pease at 0700. The Securitas gate guards carefully examined the ID cards of the two Rangers, made a radio call, then passed them through the gate to the airfield. As per the schedule, the first of the Citation business jets landed at 0800. The second, right on time at 0900. After making introductions and sharing of hugs between the sisters and cousins, everyone was loaded into the two fifteen-passenger vans for the ride back to the compound.

Once off the base, Jack and Dar pulled their vans into an empty parking lot. The Rangers then presented weapons to the two men in the new group, neither of whom were strangers to guns. Both were combat veterans. Jack and Dar were glad to have a couple more experienced shooters with them.

Twenty miles later, they were even more glad to have the extra firepower. As they approached the intersection of Route 202, near Rochester, three pickup trucks sped up the northbound entrance ramp, then stopped in the middle of Route 16.

Jack was driving the lead van. He braked hard, while shouting into his satphone. "Contact, contact, contact! Three vehicles, looks like eight tangos. We are going tactical!"

By the time Jack was stopped, Dar's van was beside him. The two Rangers and Michael's sons-in-law leaped out and took defensive positions behind the front doors, after telling the other passengers to stay down behind the seats. Michael had hardened the two vans with Kevlar door and side panel inserts and Armormax bullet-proof glass. The Master of Disasters hadn't spared any expense in preparing for situations just like this one. For this, Jack and Dar were always appreciative, but especially right about now.

The eight men behind the three pickup trucks all had long guns – all aimed at the two white vans.

One of the men shouted, "Put down your guns and walk to the front of your vehicles. Do it now!" The man's voice had the tone of authority, like that of a cop or a soldier.

Jack replied, "No fucking way, asshat. Now move your shit or lose your shit. I am not fucking with you. We will kill you all." Jack had the man's face centered in his Trijicon TR24 rifle scope and his finger resting alongside his M-4's trigger guard.

CHAPTER 18

ESCALATION

SERGEI WAS A thinking man. In his opinion, that made him one of a rare breed of men. Most, he felt, rarely actually thought about anything. They preferred to be told. His entire life – and his career – had been directed at taking advantage of this weakness in people for the good of his country. And his own self-interests, of course.

As much as he hated America and all it stood for, he admired their writers and their cinema. He learned much about their nature and their habits from this art. Sergei had always been a fan of the American writer Robert Heinlein, most especially his novella called "Gulf". He kept a dogeared page from that story in his wallet. The passage reaffirmed his views about the rest of the world.

If the average man thinks at all, he does silly things like generalizing from a single datum. He uses one-valued logics. If he is exceptionally bright, he may use two-valued, 'either-or' logic to arrive at his wrong answers. If he is hungry, hurt, or personally interested in the answer, he can't use any sort of logic and will discard an observed fact as blithely as he will stake his life on a piece of wishful thinking. He uses the technical miracles created by superior men without wonder nor surprise, as a kitten accepts a bowl of milk. Far from aspiring to higher reasoning, he is not even aware that higher reasoning exists. He classes his own mental process as being of the same sort as the genius of Einstein.

Man is not a rational animal; he is a rationalizing animal.

To Sergei, Heinlein's perspective was perfect. He had proven its truth, time and again, through the targeted use of disinformation campaigns. It was simple, really: tell someone something that conveniently fits within their own narrative, and they will not only believe that thing, but swear by it. Tell them two things, they will embrace their "convenient truth", and oppose the other "facts" – often violently. Anyone who challenges both points will be written off as an uneducated quack.

It was this logic – or lack thereof – which Sergei and his triumvirate partners were now using on their common enemy, America. They were sowing the seeds of distrust in the American government and hatred between left and right-wing groups. The perfect plan for imploding a nation – and it had been Sergei's idea.

Today, though, he had a different issue on his mind. His superiors, and those of the other members of the triumvirate, had become frustrated with the slow progress being made by Sergei and his team. Even the "inscrutable" North Koreans had expressed their impatience after the failure of the broader IOT attack on the American power grid.

His group of three had been called to a meeting in the chambers of the General Political Bureau. In no uncertain terms, the politicos wanted to know every detail of the plans developed by Sergei, Park and Bahram, including an exact timeline. As if any timeline associated with a subversive action could ever be considered "exact". Sergei called his partners via their secure phones.

"Gentlemen, are you prepared for the circus show? We have two hours before we stand in the center ring."

Park answered. "Telling that group everything is dangerous. We are spies and security operatives: they are politicians. I've never met one who could keep a secret."

"Same in my country," Bahram said. "Still, at least in Iran, if asked, we tell. The penalties for lying or obfuscating are, shall we say, 'unpleasant?' We're being asked."

"We are in agreement, my friends. Things work the same in Russia.

It's always best to deliver bad news between two elements of good news. Like that American Orion cookie."

"OREO, Sergei," Park laughed. "And they are delicious! And thank you for giving me my first laugh in months. Now, let's agree on our successes – and our less-than-successful efforts. The politicos will not be patient or tolerant."

The three discussed their efforts in attacking America from within. Their successes, at least until lately, had been many. Even before the invasion of Ukraine, Russia and North Korea had been infiltrating their enemy by embedding trained fighters, provocateurs, and saboteurs within the seemingly endless flow of illegals crossing America's southern border. Most of them were neither Russian nor Korean, but were from Cuba, Nicaragua, and Venezuela, easily blending into the massive influx of other Latin migrants.

Since the turn of the millennium, nearly a million of these stealth troops had crossed, all with forged identities that would – and in many cases had – pass even the most rigorous background check. The triumvirate hackers had been stealing identities for years. These were gleaned and vetted for ones that would be useful in support of this mission. The lazy Americans made things so easy, with their lackadaisical approach to protecting their internet activities.

The Iranians were great hackers and internet thieves, but less good when it came to sending clandestine troops. Americans were, in large part, suspicious of all Middle Easterners, making it difficult to integrate them into the social fabric.

The ridiculous way the Americans left Afghanistan changed that, however. It was, by any interpretation, a chaotic debacle. Tens of thousands of quickly assembled Afghans were evacuated to Bahrain, Germany, Kuwait, Italy, Qatar, Spain, and the United Arab Emirates to conduct processing, screening, and vetting, but the process was poorly executed. With open arms, the United States welcomed over 74,000 Afghans into their country, through their Operation Allies Welcome program. Almost 5,000 of those were Iranian Quds Force operatives.

The Great Eastern European Exodus was the most significant

event, though. Over 100,000 Russians, Belarussians, and sympathetic Ukrainians subversives were welcomed as refugees, further strengthening the forces of the triumvirate. The combined Russian, North Korean, and Iranian infiltrators were split into cells, with only a few key cell leaders knowing the locations or the leaders of the other units. Training locations had been established, and the various cells were rotated through them to develop and hone skills.

All this was preparatory. The actions against The Great Satan, as Barham called America, had only begun in earnest with the launch of Phase One of the triumvirate's four phase plan. Phase One had also demonstrated many successes. The embedded provocateurs had been the catalysts for riots, protests, and even armed conflicts, throughout the United States. The Right blamed the Left, and the Left blamed the Right. Because, as Heinlein had written, *Man is not a rational animal; he is a rationalizing animal.* Occam's Razor – the simplest solution is usually the right solution. Except, it wasn't.

The most resounding successes of Phase One were the insurrections at the refugee detention centers and, of course, the cyber-attack on the American eastern power grid. The first had resulted in numerous deaths and even more hatred between what was planned to become "warring factions" within the USA. The second had not only caused physical disruptions but had further weakened trust in America's leadership. People were dying. Pockets of anarchy were growing larger every day the power was off. Yes, these were unequivocal successes.

Then came Phase Two. Not a total failure, to be sure, but not the massive impacts that the three partners had promised their superiors. Sergei knew that he would have to spin the narrative as best he could, while still being honest and humble about the failures. Not that he or any of his team could have predicted that the Americans would actually kill the majority of their internet. That had been a bold – and very astute – move on their part.

Still, Sergei thought, is that in itself not a win for us? The action had done even more harm to the trust the Americans have in their government. Was that not our goal, after all? And certainly, the actions of the conscripted "saboteurs" – Americans duped into taking action against other Americans – could be counted as a success, could it not?

Sergei and his two partners had agreed to all they could to avoid revealing details about Phases Three and Four if they could. These were aggressive and critical stages that required careful and delicate planning. Any breach of confidentiality, any leak about these plans, would leave the Americans with no options short of a nuclear response. And that would defeat the entire point of the mission: to conquer America from within.

The meeting with the combined members of the General Political Bureau did not go well. It was like the internationally recognized question: *chto vy sdelali dla menia vie posledneye vremya?* – what have you done for me lately?

They were not interested in prior success. They demanded new, aggressive actions. Escalation. And they demanded detailed descriptions of Phase Three and Phase Four of the triumvirate's plan.

CHAPTER 19

UPPING THE GAME

ONE OF THE three pickup trucks across from them had two flags flying from the rear bumper: Old Glory and the yellow Gadsden Flag with a coiled rattlesnake and the motto "Don't Tread on Me". The man making surrender demands had been driving that truck. One of the others had a flag similar to the Gadsden Flag, but with a porcupine in place of the rattlesnake.

"Free Staters, boss." Jack spoke into his push-to-talk phone. "We can take them out, but it won't be long before word gets around. Shit will most assuredly get real. Orders?"

"Jack, I trust your judgment. Just get my family – and that includes you and Dar – back up here in one piece. Whatever that takes."

"Roger that, sir." Jack looked at Dar through the open doors of his van. Dar nodded his understanding of the order.

"Last chance, people!" the man behind the pickup truck blockade shout. "We don't want to hurt you. We only want your vans, fuel and weapons!"

"As I said," Jack yelled, "that ain't happening. Let's do this: we discuss this like civilized people and see what we can work out. No need to wind up with dead folks on this road, today. You and me, no weapons. I'll meet you halfway."

There was silence from the men behind the barricade. Finally, the man who had been doing the shouting stood, placed his rifle in the bed of the truck, raised his hands, and walked into the open road between the stopped vehicles.

"If you shoot me, I swear that all hell will rain down upon all of you!" he shouted, walking slowly towards Jack's position.

Jack stood up, making a big show of following the other man's lead. "No one from this side will fire unless someone from your side does. If that happens, I promise you, you don't know what hell is – but my team will show you!" Jack raised his hands and walked toward the other man, sizing him up as he did.

The other man was large. Easily six-four, Jack thought, and fit. Jack himself was no small man, either. Six foot two and 190 pounds of hard muscle, and agile as a cat. He held black belts in three martial arts and had proven himself in combat and on the streets. And, most importantly, he was an Army fucking Ranger. He didn't know the meaning of the word 'loser.' At least not as it applied to himself. As General Mad Dog Mattis had famously said: "Be polite, be professional, but have a plan to kill everybody you meet." Jack had such a plan.

The two men stopped when they were twenty feet apart. "Tueller distance," Jack thought. The Big Man had some training. Dennis Tueller, a former Salt Lake City police officer, had long ago proven that an assailant could close twenty-one feet in one and a half seconds from a standing start. The same amount of time it would take the average cop to deploy their service weapon.

Every cop was trained to know this, as was any soldier who was trained in close quarter battle. That included every Ranger. The difference being that Rangers were trained to be even quicker and to intercept an attacker, rather than let them close the distance on their own terms. Jack was one of the best at this skill. He was fast. But his quickness was his real advantage. His reaction time was almost supernatural. Jack drew in and slowly released a deep breath. He let his vision shift from a direct focus to a peripheral gaze. He could feel the handle of his Benchmade 119 Shane Siebert-designed Arvensis fixed blade knife pressing against the small of his back beneath his 5.11 TacTec Plate Carrier vest. It was not comfortable, but it was comforting.

"Name's Charlie," the big man said. "You?"

"Jack. I'd say, 'nice to meet you,' but… well… you get it. Who'd you serve with?"

"Pretty obvious, huh? Marine Force Recon. Fallujah. You?"

"Just an Army guy," Jack lied. "Couple of tours in The Stan. That settled, I don't think either of us wants to have survived that shit, just to die on a fucking state highway in New Hampshire, right? Let's talk."

"Nothing to talk about. We're taking your shit. But, since we've both laid our lives on the line for this great nation, I'm gonna make you a deal. You surrender your weapons, gas and one van, load all your people into the other one, then de-ass my area. How's that, bubba?"

Jack lunged, drawing his blade, point down with his right hand. One second later, his left hand grabbed Charlie by the right shoulder strap of his own body armor, pulling him forward. At the same time, Jack drove the pommel of his heavy knife into Charlie's chin. The big man's knees went weak, but Jack didn't let him fall. He spun Charlie around, facing back towards the men behind the barricades.

"You shoot, he dies!" Jack now had the tip of his Benchmade under Charlie's chin, already flowing blood from the first strike. Two sets of body armor and over two hundred pounds of meat protected him from getting shot. He liked his odds.

"Let him go, motherfucker!" one of the men shouted. "We will kill every one of you!"

Jack didn't answer. He moved back towards the two vans, half dragging Charlie along with him. He spoke softly into Charlie's ear. "Call them down, amigo, or this won't end well for you. Or them. My guess is, you're the only one of your group that's seen the elephant. My boys are all combat vets. Call them down by the time we reach my van, or I'll sever your brachial artery and let you bleed out on the road. That should take about fifteen seconds. Time's a-wastin', bubba.'"

They reached the vans. Jack shifted the eight-inch blade from beneath Charlie's chin to his right armpit. He pressed upward.

"Stand down!" Charlie screamed. "Stand down, you motherfuckers! Let them pass!"

"Good call, Charlie," Jack said. "You'll ride with us for a bit, just to keep your crew honest. One of my passengers is a trauma nurse. She can take care of your boo-boo for you. And we'll leave you ten gallons of petrol."

Charlie looked at Jack with something akin to appreciation. "I'd say thanks, but it hurts to talk. I'll say this, you're a sneaky son of a bitch. And quick, too."

Jack grinned. "That's me, Marine. One last thing – Rangers Lead The Way!"

Charlie shook his head. "Now, that puts things in perspective."

Ten miles up Route 16 North, Jack stopped the vans, removed two five-gallon Jerry cans of fuel, leaving Charlie and the cans on the shoulder of the road.

"Let's hope we never have to do this dance again, Marine," he said.

"No promises, Ranger," came the reply.

The remainder of the ride back to the compound was uneventful, other than what Jack and Dar later agreed seemed to be more intense stares from the groups they had passed on the way south. They figured calls or radios had passed along news of their recent adventures. No one had made attempts to stop them, though, and that's all they gave a hot damn about.

The greetings and welcome home at the compound were emotional and genuine. Michael hadn't seen this group of kids and grandkids for quite some time. After getting everyone settled in, he asked them to all join him the following morning to discuss the situation and to assign everyone to their respective roles.

Turning to Jack and Dar, Michael said, "Report to the conference in thirty for a hot wash on today's mission. And thank you." He shook both men's hands.

When Michael walked into the conference room, Ron looked up from the computer monitor connected to Raúl Hernandez's laptop.

"You ain't gonna believe this shit, boss. We just got a new message from our dear Tio Juan. It isn't pretty. Sounds like they are upping the game. We're going to have to call in the big dogs on this one."

"Let's hear it," Michael suggested.

"It's an unusually long message, spread across several detailed photos. Same encryption, just more of it. They've clearly bought into our story – which is good. Because they believe Raúl is still on the ins with us, they are directing him to reopen their admin accounts into our systems. They want any database records added since their access was cut off. It gets worse. They are planning something big. More than one thing, actually. They want Raúl to immediately begin using our connections to Homeland Security, monitoring for any chatter, news or directives related to suspected terror attacks.

They also want our boy to get them more exploitable contacts at the FAA and the Federal Railroad Administration. Specifically, the Railroad Administration's Hazardous Materials Division. They close by saying that the need is urgent, and that action is imminent. Nothing good in any of this, boss. The database they've already stolen from us has contact with those agencies. We can assume they've already been compromised."

"Jesus H. Christ," Michael said. "I need to call General Atwood. Shit's gettin' real."

CHAPTER 20

CHOPPERS AND TRAINS

ROBERT WATSON AND LD Ball didn't know each other existed. They certainly weren't aware that they were both serving the same nefarious master or working toward the same terrible goals. In fact, they would have hated each other.

LD, a dedicated follower of Putin's belligerent form of Russian nationalism, would have been Robert's sworn enemy. Robert, who viewed himself as a staunch "MAGA American", would have gladly shot LD on the street, like the pinko that he was. Yet, there they were, tools of the same craftsman. More like puppets controlled by the same puppet master – Sergei Alexandrovich.

LD was still connected to the internet because airports are considered critical infrastructure. Air services like his certainly weren't considered "critical", but his net connection was provided by the airport where he was based. Because of this, LD wasn't surprised when he got an email from "Uncle John", complete with an attachment containing twenty-five colorful, detailed pictures of African birds and beasts. The first image was of three grey crowned cranes, with long white, black, gold and brown feathers, heads topped with crowns of golden feathers, and bright red pouches below their beaks. The signal.

LD felt a rush of adrenalin. Uncle John had never sent so many images in a single email. This is something important. Something big, he thought. He opened the images, passing them one by one through the CAT function on his iMAC to decrypt the steganography. When he'd completely uncovered the message hidden within the pictures, LD sat back in his chair. He let out the breath he hadn't realized he'd been holding.

"Son of a bitch, is this for real?" he asked out loud. But the birds and beasts on his monitor did not reply.

Most previous messages had been short and usually a bit cryptic. This one was long, detailed and crystal clear. He had a mission. One that he might not survive: the type of mission that he'd been prepped to expect, someday. Still, that made reading it no less frightening to him.

LD felt the bile rise into his throat. He grabbed his wastebasket and puked up what had been a great breakfast of Waffle House bacon, eggs, and biscuits. Cold sweat broke out on his brow. It was one thing to say you're prepared to die for your ideologies; an entirely different thing to realize that you're about to do so. Suck it up LD, he thought. This the big game.

An appropriate analogy, considering what he'd been ordered to do.

The message from Uncle John left no room for interpretation:

Your last delivery was fifteen kilos of powdered fentanyl. You are to load it into your crop duster systems and spray it over Bryant-Denny Stadium during the football game, this coming Sunday. Thank you for your service to the Glorious Motherland. You will be remembered as a Hero!

"Fifteen kilos!" LD again spoke to his empty office. He knew the chemistry of poisons. He'd made a career of using various concoctions to exterminate pests of every nature. But this was something else entirely. Fifteen kilos of fentanyl would be enough to kill millions of people. Bryant-Denny Stadium held over 100,000 fans. This coming Sunday – three days away – was the Alabama vs Ole Miss game. Covid or not — since there were no lockdown mandates — the stadium would be filled to capacity.

LD sat still behind his desk. Three short days…

As he was boarding a city bus in Oklahoma City, Robert's cellphone blasted the first notes of "Dixie", earning him disgusted looks from the Black bus driver and several 'woke' passengers. He didn't care. That song was the alert tone he'd programmed for his WhatsApp messages. He only used that app for one contact.

"Fuck all y'all," he said to the bus occupants.

When he was in his seat – one at the rear of the bus and with no seatmate — he opened the message. It was short, like all the others: *Cherokee Motel. Pick up package waiting for you at the front desk.*

Robert pulled the cord above his seat window, signaling the driver to let him off at the next stop, where he called for an Uber to take him to the rented garage where he kept his pickup. A new-to-him used Ford F-250.

The Cherokee Motel was a "No tell Motel" in Oklahoma City West, near the airport. Not a great area, but that was cool. Robert didn't exactly fit the profile of the neighborhood. He was a large white redneck wearing a red MAGA hat and a Stars and Bars Confederate battle flag on his denim jacket. Everyone else was either non-white, or what his daddy would call 'white trash.'

It was almost 2200 hours before Robert made it to the motel. He parked his car two blocks away from the entrance to The Cherokee, where SW 5th Street curved into Westside Drive. He walked back, moving like a man on a mission. Which he was.

Between the street and the entrance to the hotel, he was greeted by two pimps, their prostitutes, a man urinating in the parking lot, and a guy trying to sell drugs. Not exactly a Five Star joint, Robert thought.

The Native American clerk behind the bullet-proof glass looked up at him. "You want a room, amigo?"

Robert laughed. "Are you fucking kidding, Cochise? Do I look like one of your crack head customers? Name is Wilson. I think you have something for me."

"Wilson" was the name Robert and his connection had agreed to use for missions like this.

"Okay, *Yo-ne-ga,* give me a minute," the clerk replied, using the

Cherokee word for white man, although the word actually meant much more. All translations of the Cherokee word for white men or white man (both male and female) are negative connotations of the same basic theme: dishonorable, liar, thief not real humans, cannot be trusted. The clerk felt that it was the right term for the man standing in his lobby today. It was a racist slur, but no worse than being called "Cochise".

The clerk came into the lobby through a door alongside the glass enclosed counter, pulling a black Pelican case. He passed the extended handle to "Wilson".

"Do I get a tip, man?" he asked.

"Fuck off, dude. I know my associates already covered you. Probably a lot better than I would have. Have a nice fucking night."

The clerk laughed out loud. "I don't see no wheels, so I guess you best be callin' your Uber. Good luck with that. Those chickenshits won't come down here, even in the daytime! You're shit outa luck, dude. You can walk the fuck back to your own side of the tracks, but you ain't stayin' here."

Robert considered punching the smartass clerk in the throat but decided against it. He had no idea what was in the Pelican case but knew that he didn't want to find out in front of a cop, assuming even the cops would come to this shithole area. He turned towards the door.

"By the way, asshole," the clerk said. "Cochise was a fucking Chiricahua Apache. I'm Cherokee. Read a book someday."

Robert flipped the man off without turning back to look at him. He walked out the door and turned right onto SW 5th Street, carrying the Pelican case in his left hand. It was heavy, but Robert was a strong man. And he didn't want to look like some wimp, rolling his carry-on through an airport.

Halfway to his truck, Robert heard footsteps behind him. As he passed a shop window, he could see a tall man in the reflection, moving toward him with a determined look on his face. The man was half a block back, walking fast. He turned his attention back to his front and saw two sturdily built Native American men step out of a doorway, thirty feet ahead of him. Robert stopped. Here we go, he thought.

"Hey, *Yo-ne-ga*, we're here to help you with your bag," one of the men in front of him said.

"You know, I've heard that word before, recently," Robert said. "Somehow, I don't think it means 'good buddy.' And I'm pretty sure that I wouldn't like whatever it does mean. Whatever. I don't need help with my bag, so why don't you boys just piss the fuck off?"

The two men in front of Robert laughed at him. He could hear the man behind him closing the distance. Perfect, he thought. He took two more long strides towards the two men in front of him, then, spinning a full turn, like a discus thrower, hurled the heavy case – at least fifty pounds, he figured – into the man now running at him from behind. The case hit the tall man at waist level.

The man tried to catch it, like a well-thrown football. Physics did the rest. Fifty pounds of hard plastic, thrown by a two-hundred-pound man – spinning to increase momentum – into a 150-pound man, running directly into it at top speed. Newtonian Physics: not just a good idea; it's the law… and it worked.

The running man was stopped dead in his tracks. He collapsed backwards onto the sidewalk, the heavy, solid Pelican case landing on top of him, still wrapped in his arms.

Robert continued his spinning turn, launching himself at the two men blocking his way. He had his Glock G19 Gen5 concealed carry pistol inside his waistband but didn't draw it. Neither of the two bad guys had flashed a weapon, though Robert assumed them to be armed. Didn't matter. Robert was on them before they got over the shock of watching him pirouette like a ballet dancer.

One of the two would-be robbers had taken two steps in Robert's direction. He was first to feel Robert's flying knee strike, taking the blow in his solar plexus. The man's breath exploded out of him with a loud *'oof'* sound, as he flew backwards into his partner.

Robert's left elbow struck the second man at the same time as the first assailant's body did. Both bad actors hit the sidewalk like two very large piles of cow shit. From the smell of it, the first guy actually HAD shit himself.

"Bad day for the bad guys," Robert said to the groaning man on the sidewalk, as he picked up the Pelican case. "Redneck three, redskins zero."

Robert made it back to his truck without further trouble. He took Westside Drive to the West I-40 Service Road, then steered onto I-40 towards Oklahoma City proper. He checked into a Hampton Inn near the junction of I-40 and I-35. He had no idea what was in the Pelican case but wasn't comfortable taking it back to his apartment. For all he knew, it could contain a tracking device. No sense taking unnecessary chances, he figured.

The first thing Robert saw when he opened the case was a warning message: STRONG MAGNETS. PROTECT WATCHES, PHONES AND COMPUTERS! The small placard was lying on top of a sheet of metal foil, which covered a layer of foam padding. Thanks for the warning, he thought, setting his Omega watch and Samsung phone across the room on the nightstand.

When he removed the layer of insulation, Robert immediately recognized what he saw: five canisters, red with black markings. The writing on them said: GRENADE, HAND, INCENDIARY, TH3, AN-M14, TIMER CONTROLLED.

Robert had used AN-M14 TH3 grenades many times in Iraq and Afghanistan. Once triggered, they burn for forty seconds at 4,000 degrees – even under water. Thermate was vastly more effective than "old-school" Thermite, Robert knew. It would burn through a half-inch steel plate and fuse the metallic parts of any object that it contacts. Badass shit, by anyone's definition. The timer-controlled version was not standard issue, however. They were exclusively in the domain of the Army and Marine Corps "Sappers" – and Navy SEALs. The timer on this model could be set from three minutes to three hours.

Below each grenade, in its own compartment of the case, were five black rare-earth magnetic bars. Each magnet was concave on one side, obviously designed to attach the grenades to their intended targets.

In another compartment was a large manila envelope. Inside the envelope, Robert found two color-code maps, labeled "Federal Railroad

Administration — Hazardous Materials Division – Hazardous Materials Transportation Routes and Schedules – CONFIDENTIAL". Along with the maps was a letter, giving Robert the instructions he was to follow, locations and timetables.

"Damn," Robert said out loud. "This will take out the entire fucking city!" He was fine with that.

Austin. The place had digressed from a great Texas party town into a left-wing shithole. Homeless people camping – and shitting – all over the downtown sidewalks, robberies in broad daylight and an uber-liberal government that turned their backs on all of it. Good fucking riddance, Robert thought.

The instructions were well thought out. The SEALs had trained him well in the arts of sabotage and this plan was solid. He was told exactly where, when, and which train his target was to be. There were drawings, showing the exact placement of the grenades on the side bearer, aimed at the axle box. These guys knew their stuff.

Along with the instructions, the manila envelope also contained an identification card from the company who operated the rail yard he was to infiltrate for his attack. The ID even had his Oklahoma driver's license photo. Robert was impressed at the capabilities of his new bosses.

The train he was to sabotage would transport tanks of liquid propane gas, sulfuric acid, and sodium hypochlorite. The expect result of derailing the train would be a massive explosion from the LPG, along with a chlorine gas cloud caused by the combination of the sulfuric acid and sodium hypochlorite.

He was to launch the attack on Sunday – just three days away. Robert felt himself getting hard at the thought of it. He sat back in the hotel room desk chair. Three short days…

CHAPTER 21

PHASES

THE LEADERS OF the General Political Bureau were not kind to the triumvirate partners. Nikolai Platonovich, the President of the Russian Federation, had criticized and roundly chastised Sergei, but had not relieved him of his duties. Won Lee Park was removed from the meeting by four North Korean soldiers. The Koreans were a harsh people when presented with disappointment. Barham had fared best of all because he had laid all blame for failures on the other two men. His hackers, he'd said, had done their jobs thoroughly and efficiently. Sergei knew that was an accurate, if self-serving, statement.

Sergei had been demanded to give a detailed description of Phase Three and Phase Four. Phase Three, he told them, was already in motion. Orders had been sent to operatives in the United States to take action three days from then, on Sunday, and continue every day for the following week. Orders that would result in the deaths of a million or more Americans.

Some, those sprayed or otherwise massively exposed to high-grade fentanyl powder, would be killed instantly. As would most of the first responders rushing to their aid. Others would die a slower, more painful death, due to exposure to toxic chemicals and gasses caused by a series of explosive train derailments. The leaders behind the large dais were visibly excited by this information.

"Explain how this has been arranged, Sergei," said Nikolai Platonovich. "Are all the materials in place?"

"Yes, *Tovarisch Predsedatel*. For years, we have been paying the Mexican Cartels to divert hundreds of pounds of their Chinese-made fentanyl to our agents. We've paid them more than they could get for the product on the streets of America, with a fraction of the risk. That uncut powder has now been distributed to a select group of twenty operatives, whom we've groomed for decades.

"For the train-based chemical attacks, we leveraged the cyber resources of Iran and DPRK to gain access to the systems that control cargo shipments and those of their human resources departments. Through these, we have assigned the types of chemicals we need to the trains we choose, for most impact on our selected targets. We used their personnel data to create identification cards and credentials for our saboteurs.

"In this case, those actually conducting the attacks are Americans who have no idea they are working for us. Pawns in our game, nothing more. Because of the complexity of the mission, there are ten such actors involved, all of whom believe that they are striking a blow in support of their own factions – some from the left, some from the right. All are former military, with experience in explosives and demolition."

"Impressive," said Choe Ryong Hae, President of the DPRK Presidium. "Still, I will withhold my applause until we see these attack work successfully."

Sergei went on to explain that the intent of Phase Three, aside from the obvious, was the bring America to the brink – if not over the brink – of civil war. "Both extreme political factions will blame the other, he explained. "Both will also deny the attacks, but the evidence we'll leave will be undeniable. And our embedded leaders within their ANTIFA and POK organizations will encourage armed responses toward the other side. When that begins, we will be ready for Phase Four."

"Phase Four is the most complex," Sergei continued. "Our forces will mobilize to their respective targets, amassing units of 100,000 fighters per unit. These are all well-trained infantry, combat engineers, medics and saboteurs. We do not have armor or artillery but will acquire them as we overrun, and defeat weakened American military bases. Our plan is to attack their National Guard bases, which are less well defended than their larger bases. Our agents already have our people inside many such facilities, working as housekeepers, groundskeepers, and other such positions.

"At the designated hour, other units will attack American seats of government, including several large state capitals and Washington, DC. The mission will be to capture their leaders – alive, if possible – and to use them as hostages in order to negotiate a surrender."

"They will fire their nuclear missiles!" shouted Kim Yo Jong. "We would do the same, under those circumstances, would we not?"

"At whom?" Sergei asked. "The majority of our embedded forces are from Latin America. They will be speaking Spanish. They will not all be in a common uniform. Their only emblems will be green armbands or green bandanas. The Americans won't even know who they are up against – until they fall."

Sergei realized that he should also share his biggest concern about the success of Phase Four: Covid BX6.5. Like the rest of the world, his forces were not immune to its ravages. Over 10,000 of his troops had died already. The virus was weakening his forces along with those of the Americans – but they had more troops to lose than Sergei did.

"We may soon have a solution to that," said Choe Ryong Hae. "We are working to leverage our mutual support agreement with our Chinese friends, to get access to their vaccine for Covid. As you know, it's the only thing that works against this new strain. They say it will work against all future strains, as well. Once we finalize the agreement, we will allocate two million doses to you. If you can get them to your embedded forces, that is."

Sergei felt a jolt of adrenalin. "Thank you, sir! I can arrange for our Cartel associates to smuggle them across the American southern border. They are proficient in doing that. Sir, this will most definitely help to ensure the success of our mission. Thank you!"

After the meeting, Sergei went to find his friend, Park. He was afraid that his Korean counterpart might have been arrested and detained, but found him in his office. Deflated, visibly shaken, but unharmed. Sergei was pleased. The two partners had much to do over the next three days.

Three short days…

CHAPTER 22

THREE SHORT DAYS

RON RIVERA FELT his stomach drop. He felt as if he would be physically ill. He didn't have a bug or another bout with Covid. It was even worse. He had just read the newly received message from "Tio Juan".

La Fase Tres está en marcha. Los primeros ataques comenzarán el próximo domingo y continuarán durante la semana siguiente. Hemos aprovechado sus datos en beneficio de la causo. Continuar monitoreando la FAA y el tráfico ferroviario para cualquier acción que tomen conocimiento de nuestras acciones. Espere más instrucciones.

He translated and transcribed the message for Michael and others to whom it would need to be relayed:

Phase Three is underway. First attacks will begin this coming Sunday and will continue for the following week. We've leveraged your data to the benefit of the cause. Continue to monitor FAA and railroad traffic for any indications that they become aware of our actions. Stand by for further instructions.

Ron almost wished his nausea WAS some disease. At least he'd have been able to take something for it. In this case, the only cure would be to stop these attacks, if that was even possible. He called Michael.

"Boss, need you down here. ASAP."

Michael read the message and immediately called General Atwood.

"General, something is about to go down," he said over his satphone. "We can't pinpoint exactly what, but we are convinced that it will be by air or rail – or both. This is not speculation, sir, it's going to begin on Sunday — three short days from now – and continue for the next week."

"Can you get more detail?" Atwood asked. "That's still a huge set of potential targets."

"We've been scouring our database, sir, using the CARVER methodology. ResourceOne had vast amounts of contact info, as you are aware. Their last message to our bogus "Raúl" has helped, though. They said that they leveraged the data he allowed them to steal. Now, we know the two likely groups – air and rail – and that they used at least some of our data to help with their mission. Rivera is narrowing his focus. I'll get back to you ASAP, but highly recommend that Homeland tighten up security for those two sectors."

"This will involve more than Homeland Security, my friend," General Atwood maintained. "If North Korea is behind a successful terrorist attack on American soil – taking American lives – it will mean war. Department of State, DOD, and the White House will need to be briefed immediately. If it comes to that, it will get ugly, quickly. You're a smart guy, Michael. Do the math. Atwood, out."

Michael's mind was racing like a Maserati. He knew the math. Regardless of what happened to the United States, South Korea would be obliterated. He and Rivera had both been assigned to the Pentagon at the end of their military careers. Both men were aware of Operations Plan 5015 to the degree that they could be aware.

What they did know was that OPLAN 5015 reportedly included an approach of limited war, through use of special forces and precision weapons to effectively decapitate the DPRK government. Cruise missiles and other guided ordnance would be used to destroy sites capable of launching nuclear missiles towards the United States, Japan and other nations. The plan projected high confidence of success – but not one hundred percent.

Under any scenario, millions of South Koreans would be killed within the first hours of the initial attack. The DPRK had thousands of rocket launchers and artillery pieces aimed at Seoul. All were capable of delivering conventional warheads and chemical / biological warheads. No plausible scenario included preventing them from laying waste to Seoul and its residents. They would be lost pawns in a nightmarish chess game.

If even a single 'KN-08" nuclear warhead equipped rocket got off the launch pad, no American city from San Francisco to Manhattan would be out of its range.

"Nightmarish." Yes, Michael thought; that's the right word.

"Ron, we've never had a more important mission in our lives. We need to figure out which of our database records fit within the air and rail sectors. Focus on the "A, V, and E" from CARVER – "Accessibility, Vulnerability, and Effect."

"I'm already on exactly that, boss," Ron said. "The air sector wasn't easy, but I feel we can eliminate actions at major airports, although we have a lot of contacts for those in our database. Our Air Evacuation Support Contracts cover over one hundred major airports, as you know. Homeland and TSA have a good handle on those, though I'd recommend heightening awareness and tightening security. As we don't have nearly as many contacts for smaller airports. we can focus our efforts there. That said, there are almost 15,000 private airports in this country, not including small strips on farms, ranches and communities. We have zero control over those.

"My recommendation, based on what we know, is to shut down all non-governmental flights for the foreseeable future. Get the FAA to send out a Notice to Airmen – they call then NOTAM – to every licensed pilot in their systems, locking them down. Then shoot down any fucking plane or chopper that flies."

"Can't be any worse than shutting down the fucking internet, right?" Michael's sarcasm was on full display. "What about the train-borne threat?"

"Thanks to 'Tio Juan' being so descriptive, I've been able to narrow my queries significantly," Ron said. "We only have twenty-five records of employees of the Hazardous Materials Division. I've put those records into your secure file folder. You should get those to the folks in DC to have them try to determine if one or more of those employees have had any unusual data transactions recently. Since they're deemed Critical Infrastructure, they are still connected to the net, which means they are still active threats."

Before Michael could respond, an email notification popped up on his Signal app. It was from NSA Deputy Director Sarah Burton. It was short, but Michael doubted it would be sweet:

Secure WebEx – five minutes – MANDATORY

Michael felt a familiar pit in his stomach - one that he'd always felt, just before a serious mission. A feeling that had served to keep him centered when everything around him was going to shit, which, he thought, things are about do.

CHAPTER 23

THE GATES OF HELL

THE WEBEX CALL had fewer participants than the last one had. Susan Hardy from DHS, General Bob Atwood and Sarah Burton from NSA, Ed Sterrett from FBI, Bobby Dunn from FEMA – most of whom would be out of work when the new president was sworn in, ten days from then – and four new participants: Senator Frank Griffith, Chair of the Senate Armed Services Committee and General Mark McGuire, chairman of the Joint Chiefs of Staff, Secretary of Defense Dan Amos, and Secretary of State Margaret Havens.

"Ladies and gentlemen, let us get started," General Atwood began. "You've all been briefed, as have the current and incoming presidents. The situation cannot be cast in any positive light. We are being forced to take swift and aggressive action against North Korea. Preemptive action, which will cost millions of lives and throw the entire world into more chaos than it is already in. A thing I would never have believed possible.

"Before we go further, allow me to introduce Michael Conrad, to those who don't know him. Michael is a decorated former Ranger. He holds a Top-Secret/SCI clearance, so is authorized to read in on any topic we choose to include him on. He is currently under contract to several agencies represented on this call. It was the work of his team members that uncovered the imminent threats we now face. I'll now turn it over to SecDef Amos."

"Thank you, General," Secretary of Defense Amos said. "Ranger Conrad, nice to put a face with the name. Thanks for your continuing service to our great nation. I wish the outcome of your efforts weren't so dire.

"Like others on this call, I may or may not be in this post after the inauguration. I almost wish that I was not in it now. But here we all sit, faced with decisions that will change the face of not just our nation, but the world. Decisions that must, however putrid, be made. I pray that our successors will be able to manage through the coming chaos. General McGuire, the floor is yours."

"Thank you, Mr. Secretary. Ladies and gentlemen, our plan is to conduct a preemptive strike on the DPRK. First targets will be launching sites for their KN-class rockets. Those are the ones we think are capable of hitting our homeland. Simultaneously, we will deliver a "shock and awe"-level attack on Pyongyang, focused on killing their leaders. That will include Russian leaders, now based in and aligned with North Korea."

"I see your faces," interjected SecDef Amos. "We know the risks of taking out the Russians. Our intel analysts do not think Russia will retaliate with nukes. Their second-tier commanders and politicians are fatigued and disgusted by Russia's failures in Ukraine and against NATO. We think they'll welcome the opportunity to stop the wars."

"Thank you," said General McGuire. "Once our initial attack is over, we will follow with special forces troops from our service branches and those of South Korea. We have already begun to move these troops onto carriers, in preparation. We're moving them now, because we are faced with the reality that once we strike first, DPRK conventional forces will immediately attack Seoul and all our bases. Most likely, the attacks will be chemical and biological in nature. Our soldiers are equipped and trained for that, but civilians are not. There will be a massive number of casualties within the first hours of the strike."

"Dear God," Susan Hardy said. "I know we can't evacuate Seoul, but can we at least issue a warning?"

"We cannot," McGuire said. "It would be strategically and tactically imprudent to even try. The only advantage we have is the element of surprise. South Korea is filled with DPRK spies. Any warning to the residents of Seoul is a warning to Pyongyang."

"What about China?" Michael Conrad asked. "Will they come to the aid of North Korea? That would be a very bad thing for us."

"Excellent question, Mr. Conrad," said Secretary of State Havens. "As it turns out, we have, for years, fundamentally misunderstood China's relationship with the Kim government. We have long believed that Beijing is committed to North Korea's survival and might take steps to ensure that the Kim regime doesn't collapse and send millions of starving refugees flowing into China.

"Based on more recent intel, we now believe that China would quickly send thousands of troops into North Korea to seize control of the country's nuclear sites and prevent Kim from using the weapons. Chinese and North Korean troops wouldn't be working together against a common enemy; they'd be trying to kill each other. Chinese troops would need to advance fewer than one hundred miles into North Korea to take control of all the country's highest-priority nuclear sites and two-thirds of its highest-priority missile sites. The catch is, we'd need to let them take Taiwan."

"The thing is," said SecDef Amos, "we can't strike them until we are attacked. What we have right now is speculative – albeit strong – data about a probable attack. We need to find the attackers, if they exist, and, with luck and the help of the Almighty, stop them before they execute their missions. If we have that proof, or — may the saints preserve us – if they are successful, then we take them out."

Everyone on the call was silent. Some were obviously praying. Finally General Atwood broke the silence.

"Ranger Mike, you've done good work. We wouldn't know what we know without your help. That said you are relieved of further involvement, other than continuing to monitor and report on communications from your sources. You have the thanks of a grateful nation. Things will get worse before they get better, I'm afraid. Good luck to you and yours. And that wish goes to everyone on this call. We are about to open the gates of Hell."

CHAPTER 24

SUNDAY

AT 0200 ON January 11th, 2025, Robert Watson pulled into a railroad switching yard, just south of Waco, Texas. The guard at the gate scanned his employee badge with a handheld scanner and opened the gate. Robert then drove to the location outlined in his set of orders. As with every mission he'd been on as a Navy SEAL, he was calm and focused. He parked his truck, picked up his black Pelican case, then walked to the side of car number 2323 – a tanker car filled with liquid propane gas.

He checked his surroundings. Seeing no one, he slid beneath the car, opened the case, removed two red canisters with black lettering on them. Using the strong rare earth magnetic mounts, he attached five of the AN-M14 TH3 Thermate grenades to the train car's axles, just as described in his orders. He set each of the mechanical timers for three hours. He placed one of the grenades in a location that aimed the bottom of the cannister at the steel tank. The thermate would burn through the thick steel in less than a minute. The explosion would be massive.

Robert repeated the process on two more cars. When they detonated, the moving train would derail. If the derailment itself didn't cause the desired effect, the exploding LPG tanker would. The timers would cause that to happen as the train reached Austin.

Lucious David Ball hadn't slept for two days. In fact, he'd not left his office at Huntsville Executive Airport. He hadn't eaten much, either. Stress has that effect on people. Especially people who were about to kill over 100,000 human beings – and die in the act of doing so.

LD had received the NOTAM on Saturday, grounding all but governmental and emergency service flights. He wasn't worried about that, though. He knew that no one would be staffing the tower at the Executive Airport until after 1000 hours on a Sunday. He would be airborne before dawn. He also knew that he could fly from his field to Tuscaloosa below the radars of Birmingham International and Huntsville.

He had planned his route carefully. He would follow back roads, rivers, and valleys, flying close to the terrain. His military and crop-dusting experience would serve him well. Probably scare the crap out of a few hillbillies and meth heads though, he thought.

LD had picked a clearing in the woods around Tuscaloosa Lake as a spot to land and wait. He would be there before sunrise. When the time was right, he would take off, pop up to an altitude of three hundred feet, and fly towards Bryant-Denny Stadium. He would be on top of them before any response could be mounted.

And that, as they say, would be that.

LD put on his HazMat suit, completed with oxygen cannister. He did a quick preflight check of his Robby R44, climbed into the pilot seat and started the engine. His hands were shaking as he pulled up on the collective, taking the helicopter to a height of twenty feet above the tarmac. Pushing the pedal under his left foot, he turned the bird west, away from the main airport buildings. He twisted the throttle handle with his right hand and eased the cyclic forward. He increased the speed, skimming just above the tarmac at 150 kilometers per hour. Once clear of the open airfield, he slowed the aircraft, to better negotiate the flight path he'd chosen.

His plan worked just as he'd expected. In just over one hour, well before sunrise, LD landed in a hidden clearing, four flight-minutes from his target. When he'd shut down the Robby's engine, there was silence. Except in his heart. And his head.

Robert sat in his truck, waiting to watch his train pull out. The schedule he'd been given indicated the wait should have been a short one. He was surprised that none of the trains in the switchyard were moving. Finally, twenty minutes after the scheduled time, his targeted train began its slow crawl down the tracks. Robert hoped the delay wouldn't lessen the effects of the explosion. That shithole of a town needs to be purged, he thought.

But there were things Robert didn't know.

On the previous evening, the Federal Railroad Administration had mandated a full stop for every train in the United States of America. The order was to remain in effect for an indeterminate period. The Administration's Hazardous Materials Division had directed every train carrying hazardous cargo to be moved to isolated sidings as quickly as possible. Robert's train was now heading for a remote railroad spur, south and west of Waco.

Robert also didn't know that when the gate guard had scanned his ID badge, alerts had gone off at the railroad regional headquarters in Ft. Worth. The name on the badge was one that the FBI had flagged as probable counterfeit. It showed as valid but was one of the employee records that had been compromised in a data breach.

When he reached the gate, Robert didn't see the guard. He saw no one, in fact. Until he stepped from his truck to check inside the guard shack. When he was clear of his truck, ten small red dots appeared on his chest. Spotlights shone on him from every direction. A voice came over a bullhorn.

"On your face, motherfucker, NOW! Hands where we can see them!"

100,000 people. More, if the first responders are counted in the mix. Tens of thousands more if the winds were just right. LD was at once sweating and chilled as having been in a cold shower. His heart was beating so hard that he could see it pulsating through his white HazMat suit. Then, like an epiphany, he knew. He was instantly calm and in control.

He would not go through with this thing. He could not go through with it.

"Birmingham ATC, this is Robinson R44 N4128L. May Day, May Day, May Day," he spoke into his radio microphone.

"This is Birmingham ATC," came the response. "What is your emergency?"

"Birmingham ATC, N4128L. I am flying a mission to conduct a terrorism strike on Bryant-Denny Stadium, today, at the direction of the Russian government. This can all be verified through a search of my office in Huntsville. Please send authorities to my coordinates. Instruct them to wear HazMat PPE. My cargo is deadly."

LD gave the controller his GPS coordinates, then turned off his radio. He waited. Within minutes, he heard the sirens. He knew the different tones – police, fire, ambulance. He waited.

When the sounds grew close to his location. LD opened the door of his beloved airship, disconnected his oxygen hose from the tank, and stepped to the back of the helicopter. He opened the filler cap on the KFlow 200 high output spray pump of the crop duster system. He put the loose end of his oxygen hose into the powder-filled tank and inhaled.

CHAPTER 25

QUIET REFLECTION

ROBERT WATSON SAT up. He wasn't sure exactly how long he'd been locked in that small cell he'd been in, but it must have been a few days. At some point, they'd come into the cell and stuck him with a needle in his jugular. Now, he was on the floor of a military airplane, with a black bag over his head. I'm being renditioned, he thought. Robert knew this because, as a Navy SEAL, he'd been involved in several such operations. From the sounds he could hear, he was on a C-130. He had not a clue about anything else. Leavenworth? Hell, Gitmo, maybe? He could call out and ask, but he knew he wouldn't get an answer.

"Gotta piss!" he yelled.

"Piss yourself, asshole," a female voice replied. "Or hold for twenty minutes until we land. I ain't unlocking your hands – and I sure ain't holding your pecker for you. If I could even find it."

"Fuck you, bitch," Robert said. "One touch of me, and that'll be the memory you giggle about when you're in the old folks' home. If you fucking live that long."

Robert leaned back against the wall, laughing. Twenty minutes later, he heard and felt the plane preparing to descend. Forty minutes later, he was on the tarmac, being forced along by two seemingly large hands, one on each of his arms.

"I really gotta piss, fellas. Either right here, or as soon as you put me in whatever vehicle you're puttin' me in. Your fucking call."

"For Christ's sakes, Wayne, shake it out for him," one of the men said, as he pulled to a stop.

Robert felt hands grab his waistband – his belt was gone – then felt and heard his zipper slide down. A cold, gloved hand reached in and pulled out his penis.

"Get it over with. Try not to piss on your shoes," the second man said.

"Thanks, brother. I wouldn't stand too close. It's fucking cold out here. Shrinkage, ya feel me?" Then Robert burst out laughing. "Ya feel me" – well, of course you did! I crack myself up, man! You can slide it back in now... but how about a friendly shake or two first?" At that, the first man started laughing.

"Fuck both y'all," the second man said, not so gently replacing Robert's member. "Let's see how funny you get up at Devon, motherfucker."

Devon, Robert thought. Old Fort Devon. He'd heard stories about the place from some of the 10th Special Forces guys he trained with at Fort Carson. He learned to do HALO jumps with those boys. They were at Devon until 1995 – long before his time in the service. What the hell was there now? Why the hell was he being delivered there?

Major General Clark Cunningham was patiently sipping a cup of black tea, waiting for his "special visitor" to arrive from Logan Airport. Around him stood six other men and two women. Two Army officers and the rest in either dark suits or "tacticool" civvies. Subtle as a neon light in a whorehouse, he thought. All the "three letter agencies" were represented. After his work at Gitmo, he could read them from across a parking lot. Of course, that was long before he had stars on his shoulders. That work wasn't often discussed in polite company. That's why he had been surprised when he got the call from his old pal Bob Atwood, asking him to do him a solid. There was a sensitive "inquiry" to be conducted and Cunningham was the best of the best at such things.

Fort Devons was a place few paid attention to, these days. No more military presence, theoretically. Since the closing of the military base, many of the existing buildings had been renovated or reconstructed;

housing developments now existed, along with a growing business park, a new hotel, restaurants, several public and private schools, a golf course… and one very special building that was owned by a 'private company' out of Foggy Bottom. That building held an anechoic chamber that had been used to test stealth fighter components for any discernible radar reflections.

An anechoic chamber is a room designed to stop reflections of either sound or electromagnetic waves. They are also isolated from energy entering from their surroundings. The one in this building was silent to -20dB. Human hearing ceases to detect sound at 20dB. It was beyond silent inside the chamber. This room was the size of a two four-car garages – assuming the garages were fifty feet tall inside. It had massive foam cones protruding from every wall and from the ceiling. It looked like the inside of some medieval torture chamber. Which, as it turned out, it had become.

The van from Logan pulled up to the front of the building. The two Marine guards helped the hooded prisoner out of the back of the vehicle and through the front doors. General Cunningham pointed the guards to a door behind what looked like a normal receptionist counter. Beyond that door was the room that housed the anechoic chamber, which itself had a door twenty feet high and three feet thick, covered on the inside with the same foam cones that covered the wall and ceilings.

In the center of the dimly-lit chamber were two heavy chairs, facing each other and bolted to the rubberized floor. Robert was placed in one of them, and his hood was removed. His wrists and ankles were strapped to the arms and legs of the specially made, rubber-coated chair he was placed in, using nylon straps. His metal handcuffs and the hood covering his face were removed. As his eyes adjusted to the soft lighting in the room, he had no idea what he was looking at.

It was a massive room, with foam spikes protruding from the walls and the ceiling. An acoustic chamber of some sorts, he thought. Robert saw a man entering the large door to the chamber. The size of the door made the man look small, at first, but as he walked to the chair across from his, he could tell that the man was anything but small.

Robert figured him to be at least six-foot six, with an athletic build, wearing the battle fatigue uniform of the United States Army, with two stars on the front along with jump wings, and both Ranger and Special Forces tabs above the 82nd Airborne patch on the shoulder of his left sleeve. A Major fucking General, he thought. This is getting curiouser and curiouser.

"No need to get up," the General said, with a grin. "We won't stand on formalities. I'm General Cunningham. You can just call me... well... General Cunningham. And your name is Mr. Robert Watkins – formerly Chief Petty Officer Robert Watkins, Naval Special Warfare Command, SEAL Team Six. We good so far?"

"Are we good? Do you see me strapped to a fucking chair, General? I am not fucking good, no," Robert replied. "And my immediate future doesn't look promising, either."

"Fair enough," The General replied. "But that last part will be up to you. You've been a bad boy, former Chief Petty Officer. I want to know all about why and for whom you've been doing these bad things. How's about you just spew forth and save us some time?"

"I'm just what y'all call a lone wolf, sir. Nothing more to report."

"Strike one. This game only allows two. So let me explain the rules a bit before you blow the next one. Look around. This is a unique room, no? It's designed for eliminating sound, to the most extreme level. When that big ass door closes, you'll feel it. The room pressure changes. It will be so dark that you'll think your eyes are closed. You'll hear the sound of your own heart beating. Some have even said they could hear their nervous system humming, but I don't buy that one. Got tinnitus? I bet you do. Most of us who've been in combat suffer from it. I'm used to mine. But in here, it will be the loudest fucking thing you hear. I've seen that alone cause men to break."

"They weren't Frogmen," Robert said. "Do your worst, General Fuckwad. Let's see what you got."

Cunningham laughed. "You guys are well trained; I'll give you that. I had the pleasure of interrogating a few of your cohort when I ran the program at Gitmo. Part of an extreme Survival, Evasion, Resistance, and Escape cycle, preparing them for a mission in Afghanistan. You know how the SERE thing works. Everyone is captured, after being nearly killed by the survival and evasion cycles. And no one – no one – ever successfully completed the resistance phase. Particularly, my interrogations."

"We all heard the stories about that. Figured it was mostly bullshit."

"Not bullshit, Robert. Not in the least," the General said. "I'm very good at my job. It was always more fun for me with the real terrorists, though. With the SEALs, I had boundaries I could not cross. With the Iraqi's and others, not so much. Like with you. No rules, no boundaries. I will say," he said, looking around the chamber, "I wish I'd had a room like this at Gitmo. Things tended to get pretty noisy down there."

"I really have nothing to give you, General Cunningham," Robert said. He was not a snitch. He believed in the cause he'd committed himself to. And, truthfully, he had very little to offer anyway, other than a few websites and WhatsApp numbers.

"You've just tried to destroy an entire city, Watkins. What causes a patriot to turn into a terrorist? Sure, you got a raw deal over that fucking vaccine shit. By the way, not everyone at the Pentagon agreed with those orders, including yours truly. But we followed our orders. I'm going to give you some private time, now, to reflect on your decisions. Maybe pipe in a bit of soft music to help you relax. See you shortly, Frogman."

The soldier got up from his chair and went out the massive door. With a soft hiss, it closed behind him. The feeling inside the room seemed to physically change. Robert had felt nothing like it. The closest thing was the pressure changes during submarine-based insertion training. It was palpable. The lights were turned off. The room was darker than any he'd ever been in.

Robert felt a wave of sensations wash over him. Sensations that were not common to him: anxiety; apprehension; and fear. Yes, it was fear. He became aware of a fluctuating series of tones. Then he realized they were coming from within his own head. It was almost screechingly loud, inside the ultra-silent chamber. Just as the General had said – it was his tinnitus!

The sound was blended with another perceived sound. Robert soon realized the new sound was his own heartbeat. He could actually hear his own heartbeat! And it was growing louder and faster by the second. Robert struggled against the straps holding him in the chair, but to no avail. He started yelling, just to drown out those other involuntary sounds.

Then, the music started. It was louder than any concert he'd ever attended. Alternating notes on a bass guitar, each note reverberating through his chest like bombs exploding. Then, the drums came in and the tones from an electric guitar and what sounded like a synthesizer. The music was foreign to him. It continued to grow, then fade, then swell again. So loud! Suddenly, a voice whispered something like "Careful with that axe, Eugene!" followed by primordial screaming. It was unnerving. It was horrendous. Then, as suddenly as it had started, the music abruptly stopped. But the terrible screaming didn't.

Because it was coming from Robert himself. The door to the chamber opened, and the lights came on. General Cunningham walked in and sat back down in the chair across from Robert.

"I've never been a fan of Pink Floyd," he said. "Strangely, I've never had one of my subjects ask for a copy of the playlist, either. Especially that song we just played for you. By the way, looks liked you've pissed yourself. That's embarrassing, isn't it? And you're all sweaty. If you're willing to be a bit more cooperative, I'll get you cleaned up. What do you say?"

Robert was disoriented. "How... how long...?"

"Oh," the General replied, "you've only been in here for around fifteen minutes. Seems longer, right? Start talking to me, or the next time will be an hour. How does that sound?"

Robert had never felt the way he now felt. He could not take another five minutes alone inside this chamber. An hour would cause him to lose what was left of his mind. His heart still hadn't returned to normal. He was fit. Athletically fit. His heart rate should quickly reduce to his normal resting rate of around fifty-eight beats per minute. It wasn't. In fact, the thought of being closed up inside the chamber again was causing it to increase.

"What do you want to know?" he asked.

For the next fifteen minutes, Robert told the General about the Proud Oath Keepers' chat rooms he was a member of. He told the officer about the WhatsApp messages he received, giving him orders for missions. He told them about every mission he'd conducted. All in support of his right-wing based efforts to fight back against what he perceived as a government that was destroying America from within.

"So, you see yourself as a 'Freedom Fighter'?" Cunningham asked. "What if I told you that you've been a tool for the North Koreans? That everything you did was being directed by them?"

"What the fuck are you talking about? This was purely domestic. I'd never be involved with an enemy nation. I'm fighting – as I always have – AGAINST tyranny, not FOR it!"

General Cunningham then filled Robert in on what had happened during the month of his solitary confinement and isolation. Robert knew nothing about the attack on Pyongyang or any of the aftereffects of that attack. He was stupefied.

"My God," Robert finally said. "Is there anything I can do about it, now?"

"There might be. We've made no announcement about your arrest. All that was released about the attack you attempted was that a train had been sabotaged in Texas, resulting in a massive and deadly explosion. The train actually did explode, by the way, but there were no casualties. With the majority of the internet shut down, there's really no way for anyone to validate what the 'official sources' put out there. We want you to try reaching back to your contacts. Try to get another mission, so that we can attempt to track them down and get ahead of whatever shitstorm is coming next."

"Did you ever consider that I might have agreed to help you if you'd have simply told me all that you just told me? That this chamber bullshit might have been totally unnecessary?"

"I guess we'll never know that former Chief Petty Officer Watkins, will we? But now we do understand each other, right? You have your limits – I don't have any limits, at all. I'll get some people in here to fix you up. Unless you'd like to request another song or two?"

"If I help you, will you cut me loose?" Robert asked.

"Not a chance," Cunningham said. "You're never going to breathe free air again, 'fuckwad,' but at least you might be able to redeem some of your self-respect."

Robert dropped his eyes to stare at the floor. He'd never expected to admit defeat, especially to himself, but here he was, defeated, broken, and sitting in a puddle of his own piss. How had he been so stupid? His desire for payback against a government that he felt had screwed him over had blinded him. To learn that he'd been duped by a foreign country was crushing to him.

Sure, he'd committed the acts. Terrorism was terrorism, foreign or domestic. But, to his mind, they were vastly different things. Above all else, he was an American. Even though it wouldn't help his own outcome, he knew that he wanted to help.

"I'm in," he said. "What's your plan?"

"You received a new WhatsApp message on your phone yesterday. That's why we've had the pleasure of meeting each other today. We want you to get busy."

CHAPTER 26

A PYRRHIC VICTORY

THE FIRST DAYS following the apocalyptic first strike on the Korean Peninsula were even worse than expected. The DPRK had fired thousands of VX nerve gas-filled artillery shells into Seoul, Inchon, Daegu and Buson. All the American military bases were struck, the worst being Camp Stanley, close to Uijeongbu and the nearest base to the DMZ.

The Chinese were slow in executing their attack, allowing the DPRK time to launch several rockets towards Japan. The damage to Tokyo was terrible. The only saving grace was that the missiles were armed with conventional, rather than nuclear or biological warheads.

America and her allies had been successful in their stealthy first strikes. Government and military facilities in and around Pyongyang were obliterated, as were the launch bases for North Korea's long-range ballistic missiles.

No major American city had successfully been attacked, but the leaders in Washington, DC had acted anyway. The intent had been there, they reasoned, and the attacks were only foiled through luck and solid research. The train attacks were stopped only because Ron and Michael had determined which of the Federal Railroad Administration employee accounts had been compromised. That information helped to thwart over a dozen sabotage attempts in the same way it had stopped Robert Watson.

Some trains exploded, but with little impact because they'd been moved to safer locations. In some cases, the saboteurs were killed while trying to execute their plans. A few of them were captured while trying to access their targeted trains. Based on the results of intensive interrogation, none of the would-be perpetrators knew that Russia and North Korea were behind their actions.

They believed they were "striking a blow against the man" in the name of their respective causes — some from the extreme left and some from the extreme right. All were shocked to learn they'd been duped. Like Robert Watkins, a handful had agreed to help the government in their attempts to thwart future attacks.

The fentanyl attacks were the most significant catalysts for action against the leadership in North Korea. The revelations and admissions of Lucious David Ball sealed that decision. Thanks to his early morning pre-suicide confession, no other airborne attack had made it further than a few miles from their takeoff locations. The US Airforce had deployed AWACS planes, Predator drones, and satellite systems to look for low-flying aircraft near major cities. Every major outdoor event had been canceled.

A few of the saboteurs had been shot down by drone-fired Hellfire missiles, resulting in several small communities blanketed by clouds of powdered fentanyl. There were few survivors in those towns. Most, though, had been forced to land by local police helicopters or military assets. Under 'specialized' interrogation, the pilots were determined to be Russian sleeper agents.

What no one in the US government knew about were the other attacks that had been planned by Sergei Alexandrovich, head of the Russian Fifth Service. Sergei had been killed in the initial attack on Pyongyang, along with the top leadership of North Korea and Russia. On the day of the American attack, Sergei had been preparing to execute the last element of his Phase Three plan – to use OnStar to disable vehicles all across America – then move on to Phase Four of his plan: to engage in ground attacks on important targets within the United States. The first American cruise missile put an end to all that.

None of his nearly one million saboteurs and provocateurs embedded within the borders of the United States had been given all the details of Phase Four of Sergei's plan. Without his leadership and his orders, always sent through combinations of WhatsApp messages and encrypted emails, the leaders of the insurgent cells had only their original orders to fall back on: create havoc, foster anarchy, and harass the enemy whenever and however possible. Missions that they knew, understood, and were adept at executing.

Even those missions had become difficult to coordinate as a result of the American decision to use the internet "kill switch" to shut down most of the net. Even WhatsApp had become less reliable because of the saturation of the cellular networks, nationwide. Difficult and challenging – but not impossible. The cell leaders were dedicated. They continued to find ways.

Millions of South Koreans and thousands of American service members had died in a matter of hours after the initial attack on Pyongyang. The protests and anarchy inside of America drastically increased. Air and rail supply chains were frozen, because of fears of further terrorism. Attacks on critical infrastructure, including power stations, highways, and oil pipelines, were an everyday occurrence. Barges on the Mississippi River had been commandeered and then used to ram into major interstate highway bridges, cutting off a significant share of cross-country travel.

The "victorious" attack on North Korea – and by default, Russia — proved to be the definition of "Pyrrhic" in its outcome: a victory that inflicted such a devastating toll on the victor that it was tantamount to defeat. Still, in the minds of those in power, it was a matter of choosing the lesser evil. Had they not struck first, most decision makers believed that North Korea and Russia would do so, probably with nukes. Not that second guessing mattered once the United States launched those first cruise missiles.

CHAPTER 27

DON'T TREAD ON ME

MICHAEL LAY IN his bed, thinking about all that had happened over the past six months. No one could make this shit up, he thought. One month had passed since the attack on Pyongyang. America was now hated by the entire world. No one wanted to listen to the logic of why a preemptive attack was necessary.

People both outside of and from within the borders of the United States were threatening violent retribution, and in many cases, acting on those threats. The United Nations had withdrawn their forces, leaving tens of thousands of refugees to fend for themselves inside compounds all across the country. The nation was in chaos, and anarchy was the only remaining rule of law.

But that was outside the fences and gates of his one-hundred-acre compound in the White Mountains. Inside those well-protected barriers, Michael, his family, and his team members were safe and secure. He had lived a life of preparedness. He was never sure what event might make all his efforts relevant, but he had always been convinced that it was coming, eventually.

What came, however, was more terrible than even he could have envisioned. Not that the "what" mattered all that much. All that mattered was he was prepared for almost anything. He had not been lazy. He had not been complacent.

"Good morning, people!" Michael said cheerily as he walked into the large dining area. "What's for breakfast!"

"The usual, Dad," said Andrea. "Oatmeal and fruit for you, me, and the other vegans. Scrambled eggs and venison sausage for the carnivores!" Andrea was "the organizer" of the family. One of Michael's twins, she thrived in the minutiae of planning and coordinating activities. She called it "herding cats", and she was excellent at it.

Michael grinned. "Well, you know, breakfast is the..." He was cut off before he finished his comment by a chorus of his kids' voices.

"...the most important meal of the day!" they said in unison.

Some things will never change, he thought.

Each of Michael's "invited guests" – his kids, their spouses, and Joy's sister B and her husband, Larry Katz – had unique skillsets. Nurses, an optometrist, a specialist in animals and veterinary medicine, athletic trainers, organizers, cooks, gardeners, outdoorsmen, carpenters, welders, mechanics, and electricians. All the men except Larry were combat veterans.

Most of the women could out-shoot them. Martial arts and self-defense had been fundamental in the Conrad family, since the kids were old enough to stand up. Added to the skills of the professional warfighters employed at the compound, Michael was confident in their ability to survive for as long as necessary.

As he finished his first cup of coffee, Michael got a call on his two-way radio: "Eagle One, this is Eagle Three. Need you in the SOC, ASAP."

Michael used his bicycle for the short ride to the Security Operations Center, in the compound's Command Bunker. The SOC was staffed 24/7, and housed monitors for each of the security systems that protected the property. Dar Bending – Eagle Three – was sitting in front of the large array of monitors, showing the feeds from cameras spread around the compound. One display had been zoomed-in larger than the others.

"We have a visitor at the north gate, sir," Dar said, pointing at the monitor.

There was an older pickup at the gate, with a white flag flying from the radio antenna. There were two more flag staffs on the back of the truck, one with an American flag, the other flying the yellow "Don't Tread on Me" Gadsden flag. A lone man, in tactical gear but apparently unarmed, stood in front of the truck.

"Looks like the guys we had trouble with when we went to pick up your kids."

"What's your business?" Michael asked, speaking into the intercom microphone. "Speak up. We can hear you from there."

"Name's Charlie Fernall, leader of the Free State Militia. I want to speak with Colonel Michael Conrad."

"You are speaking to him," Michael answered. He hadn't used his former rank for quite some time. Charlie's done his homework, he thought. "As I asked before, what's your business?"

"Can we speak face to face, like honorable men?" Charlie asked. "I prefer to look a man in the eye when I talk to him."

Michael turned to Dar Bending. "Deploy the RoboGuard unit nearest the gate, fully armed. Call Jack, then the two of you ride with me down to the gate to meet this guy."

The three men rode to the gate in one of the several four-seater electric carts within the compound. All were well-armed. The automated RoboGuard was already on station. Though Charlie could not tell, the robot had a 12-gauge shotgun aimed at the man's chest. Jack stopped the cart thirty yards from the gate. Dar immediately took a cover position behind the vehicle and scanned the surrounding trees through the scope of his M-4 rifle. Seeing nothing of concern, he trained the weapon on Charlie's head.

"Well, hello, Jack," Charlie said. "I had a feeling we'd cross paths again."

Jack did not speak. He stood four steps behind and to the right of his boss, his M-4 held in a 'port arms' positions across his chest – cocked, locked, and ready to rock.

"Mr. Fernall, please address your comments and questions directly to me. I'll ask this for one last time. What's the nature of your business here?"

"Calm down, Colonel Conrad," Charlie said. "I'm here to discuss the possibility of an alliance between you and the Free State Militia. We are growing stronger every day. We'd prefer you combine your resources with ours. Peacefully. How do you feel about that?"

"Not interested. You can leave now. Don't come back."

"So be it," Charlie said, raising his hands in a placating gesture. "I had to try." Looking at Jack, he said, "See ya around, partner. I owe you a dance."

Michael and his team watched Charlie get into his truck and back down the long drive. Dar never took his sights off the man, even as he drove away.

"You know this ain't over," Jack said. "He'll be back. With friends."

"No doubt. We'll be ready when they do. Let's get everyone armed up and discuss defensive strategies."

Back at the main house, Michael and his team called everyone into the dining room for a meeting. They told about the chat with Charlie and what was expected next. The compound had well-designed defensive positions, coordinated to provide overlapping fields of fire. One long side of the property was along a 200-foot cliff, providing a relatively secure natural barrier against all but the most accomplished attackers.

Michael's property extended two acres beyond the base of the cliff, and like the rest of the compound, the outer perimeter below the cliff was encircled with a twelve-foot hardened steel chain-link fence with razor wire on top, shaker sensors woven into the fence fabric, and a Senstar RoboGuard rail-mounted defensive system. In the ground on both sides of the fence were sensitive vibration sensors. If anyone attempted to climb the cliffs, there would be plenty of warning…and hell would rain down on the poor souls.

The remaining three sides of the compound were designed with natural barriers that would force any intruder to pass through "kill zones" before getting near the house or outbuildings. Michael had Claymore-type mines strategically placed in these zones. The mines would be remotely activated, when needed, with a code that only he, Jack, and Dar knew.

Michael was a firm believer in the concept of Crime Prevention Through Environmental Design and had engineered his compound with those principles in mind. CPTED, to him, was just good old-fashioned common sense. Natural surveillance, proper lighting, access control, well-placed barriers, and defensible spaces. Check, check, and double check. Add in the three modified Matrice 300 RTK drones with infrared cameras and the security net was as good as they get.

Yes, Michael and his crew were ready. He didn't relish the idea of having to defend his family and the compound through violent action, but he was prepared to do so. As was everyone inside the fences. He had made every foreseeable arrangement. He had not been, as most of the people outside his fences were, complacent.

He thought about the flag flying from the back of the guy called Charlie's truck. The Gadsden flag. Michael was born in the town of Gadsden, Alabama. The town was named after Col. James Gadsden, son of Brigadier General Christopher Gadsden, the Revolutionary War hero for whom that flag was named. He'd always loved that yellow flag and the sentiment it expressed. If it hadn't been commandeered by the extreme right as a symbol of their cause, it would fly on Michael's own flagpole. Still, in his attitude about defending his family, his home, and his country, the motto summed his feeling perfectly: "Don't Tread on Me." Indeed, General Gadsden, he thought. Indeed.

CHAPTER 28

FIRST ASSAULT

IT WAS A pristine winter's morning. Mount Washington's snow-capped peak was beautiful to behold. The air was so clean that the abandoned weather observatory on top of the mountain was clearly visible to the naked eye. There was not a cloud in the bright blue sky. But there were other things up there. Two drones. One of them – the one launched by Michael's Rangers — was hovering over the compound at about 2500 feet. Above what was once the legal attitude, but that was then, and this was now. The second, smaller drone was flying at around 1000 feet. It did not belong to Michael. It had been detected by Michael's drone, which was now tracking it.

"Eagle One, this is Eagle Four. Tracking a drone over the north sector, sir. It looks the size of a Mavic-class machine. Standing by for orders." 'Eagle Four' was the radio call sign for Ranger Nick Smith.

"Take it down, Nick," Michael replied.

All of Michael's drones were payload capable, and all carried a light-weight nylon net as a part of their kit. Nick had designed this solution specifically for taking down other drones. He could hover above the offending bird, then drop the net into its props. Game over. In this case, though, the net wouldn't be needed. The Mavic-class drones were small and fragile.

The Matrice was huge and rugged. Nick locked onto the smaller

161

drone, then slowly lowered the Matrice until it was directly above it. With a quick tap of his controller's joystick, he dropped one of the Matrice's landing gears into the propellers of the smaller drone, causing it to flip over and crash to the ground.

"Threat eliminated, sir," Nick said into his radio. "I'm going higher to scan the area for the operator. Those small drones have a range of just over four miles and standard flight time of around twenty-five minutes. In this cold, thin air, both would be drastically reduced. I'm guessing the controller is very close to us. The bird came in from the north side, so I'm thinking they will be in that direction."

"Copy that. Let's get the rest of your team to defensive positions. Arm the RoboGuard for lethal response mode, too."

Michael had been enjoying a hot cup of coffee in his sunroom, looking out over the Presidential Range of the White Mountains. A gorgeous view on a day like today, he thought. He walked back into the large dining room, where his family was sitting down for breakfast.

"Things might get interesting," he said. "Finish your chow, then get the kids to the safe room downstairs. Get your weapons and join me in the bunker as soon as you're ready."

Michael walked to the command bunker, which housed a radio room and the security operations center. Dar and Nick were scanning security system monitors and the video feed from the drones. Nick had launched a second Matrice, to cover more of the area surrounding the compound. Ron was wearing a headset, speaking with someone over the HAM system.

"We're about to have company, sir," said Nick. "There are ten vehicles strung out along the road the leads up from Route 302. At least thirty to forty tangos that we can see. Plenty of firepower. No crew-served weapons we can see, though. That's a good thing."

"Roger that, Ranger Nick," Michael said. "Are they concentrated or dispersed? Ragtag, or tactically sound formations?"

"They're spread along the northeast section of the wire, sir," said Dar. "Laying back in the woods, so far. They aren't acting like amateurs, sir. We've sent Jack and Major Tom forward to a shooting station nearer the fence."

"Major Tom" was retired Ranger Major Tom DeAngelo, the fourth of Michael's groundsmen. He was the only one of the crew who didn't have an Eagle radio call sign. Michael never passed up an opportunity to use the famous line from David Bowie's song, A Space Oddity. He picked up his radio.

"This is ground control to Major Tom," he said, causing the three other men in the room to giggle like school kids.

"Really, boss?" came the reply. "Yours may be the last voice I hear, and you're going to fuck with me?"

"Why should today be any different, Ranger?" Michael replied. "We have the bad guys on camera. You and Jack will be less than 100 yards from the fence, and they are about fifty yards beyond it. Ron and I will cover you from the roof of the main house. If they concentrate fire on your position, you two execute a tactical peel maneuver, back to the firepit. The boulder there will give you good cover."

"Just the way we've trained," said Jack. "We're good, sir."

Dar thumped his chest with the palm of his hand. Ron and Nick joined in. Michael got it. They were making a noise like a helicopter rotor, slapping the air. He knew he was being a bit of a 'Helicopter Dad,' hovering over his crew. It was just his nature.

"Let them operate, Papa Bear," Ron said. "They know their shit and they understand their commander's intent. We've got our own jobs to do."

Michael smiled, a bit sheepishly. He also knew that Ron was right. He was about to say it, when the door opened, and his family of warriors came into the bunker, all dressed in body armor and tactical gear, weapons hanging from their slings. He felt that same need to be protective rising inside again. While Alec, Ace, Gary, Ron, and Jeff were all combat tested, his wife and daughters had never fired a weapon in anger. He knew they would today. And that was a sad thought.

No person is ever the same after taking a human life. Never. The thing about surviving in combat, though, was to act now; process the emotions later. Amanda and Jessica, the two nurses, had made careers of dealing with trauma and making instantaneous life or death decisions.

Joy had been an EMT. They had seen human bodies ravaged by gunfire, knife fights, car wrecks. Andrea, Alison, Laura, Lexi and Cat had no such experiences to fall back on. But they were strong women, fiercely protective of their families – and exceptional shooters.

Michael knew that his seven kids and their spouses were smart, capable, and well trained in the arts of shooting and self-defense. Added to his team of four Army Rangers and his friend Ron Rivera, he was confident in their ability to defend the compound from the Free State Militia or any other threat. That knowledge did nothing to keep him from wanting to keep them from the shit they were about to face. He turned to face them.

"You all know your jobs and positions. It's only that – a job. Stay focused. Shoot to kill. If you wound your enemy, and that person survives, they will be pissed. They will want revenge. If you kill them, not so much. And there's a good chance you'll demoralize the person standing next to them. Based on what Ron was able to learn through chatting with other HAM radio operators, the Free Staters have been growing in numbers and strength, and their violent raids have become more frequent and ruthless. I've spent years preparing for this day, knowing that the compound would eventually become a target. It begins today but I know it won't end today."

The compound's perimeter alarms blared. The Free Staters had encroached onto the ground sensors outside the fence.

"Alright, everyone," Michael began, his voice steady and confident. "Our primary goal is to protect this compound and everyone inside it. We've trained for this, and I believe in each and every one of you. Let's show these assholes that they've picked the wrong place to attack."

The group nodded in agreement, their faces a mix of determination and resolve. They moved to their designated positions, ready to defend what was theirs.

As the Free Staters charged the wire, Michael's team sprang into action. The two forward Rangers began shooting, providing expert cover fire while the others picked off approaching enemies with their rifles. Michael and Ron Rivera, both seasoned fighters, ran to their positions on the roof of the main house. The tallest of the several structures, it provided a commanding view of the property in every direction. From there, the two senior Rangers could see all of Michael's team members and if necessary, provide them with cover fire from their scope-equipped heavy rifles.

The battle raged for over an hour. The Free Staters were relentless in their assault. Two groups of the insurgents tried using acetylene torches to breach the fence. The RoboGuards took out two of the attackers. Michael and Ron shot four more. Ron put a well-placed round into one of the gas tanks, causing a fiery explosion that killed two others. Michael's team held their ground, their training and teamwork proving to be invaluable. Finally, the attackers lost their momentum, as their casualties mounted.

Seizing the opportunity, Michael ordered a counterattack. His team charged towards the fence, weapons firing. The Free Staters, surprised by the counterattack, faltered. Exhausted and demoralized, the remaining attackers retreated into the woods, leaving behind casualties of their failed assault.

"Eagle One, Eagle Four. They're haulin' ass, sir."

"Copy that, Eagle Four. Everyone take a cover position and hold fast. I want to be sure they aren't playing us."

Michael waited a full twenty minutes before ordering everyone back to the bunker. Back inside, they hugged each other, eyes filled with relief and pride. They had fought bravely and done their jobs. Amanda and Jessica stood up.

"Dad, there are wounded people out there," Amanda said, "and we've got to help them."

CHAPTER 29

REGROUP

"WE'RE HERE TO treat the wounded!" Jack yelled, as he, Tom, Jessica and Amanda went through the gate. "If one of you fuckers reaches for a weapon, we will kill you where you lay!"

Tom and Jack went first, shielding the two nurses as they would when conducting any other VIP protection detail. They secured the weapons dropped by the insurgents, tossing them away from the wounded men and women they encountered.

The two medics moved cautiously, their hearts pounding as they approached the dead and wounded insurgents. The tension in the air was palpable, the acrid smell of gun smoke and blood filling their nostrils. Jack and Tom flanked them, weapons ready, their eyes scanning the surrounding woods for any potential threats.

As they reached the first injured insurgent, Jessica couldn't help but think of the recent battle they'd just so fiercely fought against these people. She and her sister had become nurses, following in their mother's footsteps, driven by a shared sense of duty and a desire to save lives. Appropriate, as they were both DNA relatives with none other than Florence Nightingale: the Lady with the Lamp and medical hero of the Crimean War. They had never imagined they would find themselves in a situation like this, tending to the wounds of those who had just tried to kill them and trying to patch up human beings that they themselves may have shot.

Amanda glanced over at her sister, sensing her unease. "Remember," she said softly, "our oath was to provide care to all those in need, no matter who they are."

Jessica nodded, taking a deep breath to steady herself. She knew Amanda was right; their duty was to save lives, not to judge their patients. With renewed determination, she focused her attention on the task at hand.

The nurses worked quickly and efficiently, their training kicking in as they stabilized each patient, then covered them with Mylar 'Space Blankets' to ward off the January cold. The Rangers kept a close eye on the scene, ensuring the women's safety as they administered what aid they could.

Despite the danger, the caregivers felt a sense of pride in their work. Even in the face of adversity, they were upholding the values of their profession, providing care and compassion to those in need.

As the last insurgent's wounds were treated, the responders shared a weary smile, knowing they had done their duty. As they gathered their trauma kits and prepared to return to the safety of the compound, one of the Rangers spoke up.

"I know it can't have been easy for the two of you," he said, his voice gruff but tinged with admiration. "But you did the right thing. You should be proud. I know your father and your husbands certainly are."

The three women exchanged glances, feeling a sense of camaraderie not only with each other but also with the Rangers protecting them – and with whom they'd just fought alongside. They had faced a difficult decision, but in the end, they had honored their commitment to saving lives, no matter the circumstances.

The sisters gave each other a high-five, then fist-bumped the two Rangers. They had stabilized six of the wounded insurgents. Two others were beyond saving but they were given Fentanyl 'lollipops' to stop their pain.

"Thank... you," a weak voice said. "Thank you for saving us."

Others of the Free Staters made whatever gestures of appreciation they could muster. "May God bless you both. I'm so sorry for what we tried to do."

"Are you going to leave us out here?" another asked. "We'll freeze to death before morning."

Tom responded with, "Our boss is already on it." He added, "Shut up, suck it up, and wait. At least you will not bleed out in the fucking snow. Welcome to the realities of combat, shithead."

Tom wasn't lying to them. Ron Rivera had put the word out over the HAM network about the battle, its outcome, and that aid had been rendered to the wounded. He'd asked that anyone with Free State Militia contacts have one of their leaders reach out via HAM to arrange retrieval of their wounded members. Within minutes, the radio call came in.

"This is Charlie Fernall, the leader of the Free State Militia. I want to speak directly with Colonel Michael Conrad."

"Conrad here. And I'm doing the talking. Your band of idiots paid a high price today. I hope a lesson was learned. As a combat veteran and Marine, I would have expected better from you. Your "soldiers" – and I use the term loosely – were undisciplined and ineffective. Aside from being bad fighters, they committed the greatest of combat sins: they left fellow troops in the field. I know plenty of Marines, Charlie. None would have allowed that."

"Sir, if I may…" Charlie said.

"You may not fucking say!" Michael said, interrupting the man. "What you can do is send a team up here to retrieve your wounded and your dead. My medics have done what they could. Be thankful that we, at least, are honorable. Regardless of their deluded sense of right and wrong, your militia are Americans, just like us. Come get them before they freeze to death. Our gunsights will be locked on to everyone you send, but we will not fire unless we are fired upon."

"Thank you, Colonel," Charlie finally said. "my teams are leaving now."

"And Charlie, you need to come with them. You and I need to have a man-to-man chat."

By the time the radio call had ended, the response team was back to the bunker. Michael hugged them, holding on for a long moment, proud of what they'd been conscientious enough to do.

"As soon as I meet with this asshat, Charlie, I want everyone who was involved in the armed response to meet me in the dining room for a hot wash about what happened. You all need to get it out of your minds while the feelings are still fresh. It sounds tough. It will be. But it's the best therapy. I'll find you when it's time. For now, go get hydrated and rested."

All the immediate family members returned to the main house to check on the kids and get refreshed. Larry stayed in the command bunker, so that he could relieve Dar at the security monitors. Dar and his rifle might be needed at the gate, if Charlie had any tricks up his sleeve.

Nick said, "I spy with my little eye in the sky, three trucks coming up our road. One pickup in the lead, definitely our former Marine buddy. Two vans, obviously for their wounded and dead comrades. ETA our gate, thirty seconds."

Michael, Dar, Tom, and Jack jumped into the four seat ATV and headed for the north gate. As before, Dar hopped out early, this time with fire support from Tom. Jack stopped again at the gate and, as he had before, assumed a position of cover behind the ATV. Michael approached the gate with his Sig P-226 SAS in his right hand, locked and cocked. Seconds later, Charlie's truck pulled in, again flying his white flag.

"May I approach the gate?" Charlie asked, both hands extended to show that he had no weapons in them.

"You may. Right up to the gate, past the bollards. I want to see your eyes," Michael said.

"Colonel, it's important that you believe what I'm about to tell you," Charlie said. "This was not supposed to go down like this. I gave explicit orders to probe your defenses NOT to attempt an incursion of any kind. And most definitely not to engage in a firefight. One of my wannabe warriors decided to be a 'Hot Shot Johnny' and do things his own way."

"I hope the fuck you've dealt with that motherfucker, Mr. Fernall.

His actions put my family and friends in harm's way. That won't fucking stand, amigo."

"You won't have trouble from that puke again, sir. He's laying right over there with half his head blown off," Charlie said. "And I don't want to have to do this again, either. Unless we have no other choice. You and your people showed everyone that you're good, honorable Americans. Your medics saved most of the ones they worked on, and we appreciate it. Their families appreciate it. And your crew are clearly battle-worthy. You just don't have enough of them if things get real."

"Charlie, ask your survivors how 'real' things got today. Your dead? Well, they kinda speak for themselves, don't they? Let me make this clear, amigo. It's taking every ounce of my self-control not to blow you away, right now. Or put this pistol away and just kick your fucking ass myself."

"Easy, Colonel. You don't want a piece of me. Young Jack over there was one thing. Your old ass would get hurt," Charlie smirked.

"That 'old ass' taught me to fight better than the Army did, dickhead," Jack shouted. "My money's on him. I'll give you fifty-to-one odds, too."

Charlie laughed. "We'll have to take a raincheck on that playdate, Colonel," Charlie said, with a sweep of his arm towards the people carrying dead and wounded to the waiting vans. "Besides, we're currently more concerned with the "massholes" than with your compound."

"Massholes? Isn't that the New Hampshire term for tourists and second homeowners from Massachusetts? What's the problem, there?" Michael asked.

"It's not those massholes we're concerned about. Most of the tourists are in the shelter over in Conway or refusing to leave whatever rooms they had booked. The homeowners are paying the pittance I've asked of them, in return for our protection. A few, like you, have stood up armed resistance. We'll deal with all of you standouts when and if we need to," he said. "Our intel indicates a large group of marauders heading north from the Boston area. Everyone thinks it's safer in the mountains, I guess. These are the serious massholes. They've taken anything they want as they passed through some of the smaller towns down south. Not without plenty of resistance, though. Many killed on both sides. Intel says they are heading up here to the Whites."

"I appreciate that information, Mr. Fernall. And as for the raincheck… a sunny day will work just as well. Clean up your mess and de-ass my property," Michael said, mounting the ATV.

That's just spiffy, Michael thought. He'd never liked the term "masshole" – in this case, it sounded more appropriate. He needed to get his team regrouped and ready, when and if more fools tried to take their new home from them. He appreciated hearing that a few other up here had told the militia to piss off. He was pretty sure he knew who a few of them were. It was time to make some alliances of his own.

CHAPTER 30

USE IT OR LOSE IT

BAHRAM MOHADJER WAS at his desk inside the Tehran headquarters of the Basij Cyber Council. It had been one month since the American strike on Pyongyang. He was still surprised by the Chinese response. He hadn't expected that they would come to the aid of the Americans. It was more than disconcerting for him because the Chinese had been read in on almost every action taken by the triumvirate. If the Chinese share what they know with the Americans, they will surely nuke us, Bahram thought.

Bahram had convinced the leaders of the Quds Force to go onto high alert status. His cyber warriors were tracking constant chatter about a preemptive attack from the Zionists, just as the Americans had done to his two partners. Iran could not prevail in that fight, regardless of the Ayatollah's blustering. It was true that Iran has a few tactical nukes, thanks to his former Korean and Russian partners, but no way to deliver them. They had not been modifiable to fit in the cones of the Iranian medium-range missiles. Still, even those missiles could reach beyond the West Bank.

There was no way to know when his time would be up. He was fearful and frustrated but had one last blow he could strike against The Great Satan – the last element of Phase Three of the triumvirate's plan. Attacking the American's OnStar system, adding more salt to their bleeding wounds. Bahram wished he could personally launch Phase Four of the plan, but he had no means to do so. He did not have the command authority or the contacts inside of the United States to reach out to. So, he would do what he could.

Barham called his Basij hacker force team leader.

"Hit the OnStar System at 1630 PDT tomorrow. There are fewer cars running now than before the grid attacks, but that time of day will be busy in all four of their time zones for those that are on the road. It's all we have left. We use it or we lose it."

The convoy of randomly acquired vehicles rolled north on New Hampshire Route 16. Inside the vehicles and in the backs of the trucks were the ragtag collection of gangsters and miscreants that had banded together to loot, sometimes rape, and generally pillage every store and home between Boston and the White Mountains of New Hampshire.

The gaggle was led by Ed Flannigan, a career punk from Roxbury, in South Boston. When the power went out and it became clear it would be out for a long time, Flannigan gathered some of his pals and began looting and robbing. And killing when things didn't go their way.

By the time the USA attacked North Korea, Flannigan had amassed a small army of over two hundred mostly younger men and women who decided it was easier to take what they wanted instead of waiting for government handouts. Because of the American attacks, Flannigan and his cohort, calling themselves New Southies – a nod to "old school" gangs like the Mullen Gang and the infamous Winter Hill Gang once run by Whitey Bulger – were convinced that a nuke would soon fly toward Boston. Their plan was to head into the safety of the mountains, taking everything they wanted along the way.

The New Southies had avoided the bigger towns as they moved north – those that might still have more than a handful of cops with guns – sticking to local roads rather than interstate highways. They had generators with them to power pumps to steal gas from the underground tanks at gas stations. What they needed, though, were more vehicles to carry their growing band of marauders. They hit paydirt at an abandoned GM dealership in Exeter, New Hampshire.

With ten new Chevy pickups and six new SUVs in their army, they'd taken Route 27 out of Exeter towards Route 125. Their maps told them that road would take them to Route 16 North. As they drove along Route 27, Flannigan saw the entrance sign for the Sig Sauer Academy and Pro Shop on his left. He screeched his new Tahoe SUV to a halt. Two paydays today, he thought. Hallelujah!

The end of the driveway to the Sig Academy was guarded by two men in tactical clothing and carrying rifles. When the guards saw the number of guns they'd have to overcome, they put their weapons on the back of the truck they were standing behind and raised their hands in surrender. Ed Flannigan walked up to the two men with a smile on his face, then shot them both.

Looting stores in and around Boston had taught the New Southies lessons. They had all the tools they needed to cut through the steel security shutters on the windows of the Pro Shop and the range. In a matter of thirty minutes, they had filled trucks and SUVs with a cache of weapons and ammo.

"Sig Sauer," Flannigan said, brandishing his new M400 Tread rifle. "Never Settle!"

The hoard remounted their trucks and headed north, to 'conquer more lands' as Flannigan had told them.

Twenty miles after getting onto Route 16 North, just beyond a point where, just a few weeks earlier, a former Ranger had embarrassed a former Marine, things went weird.

At exactly seven-thirty PM, every one of their new GM vehicles went dead, along with every other OnStar-equipped car in the United States of America.

Back in Tehran, Barham had no way of knowing how effective his cyber-attack had been. The lack of internet access in America had taken a heavy toll on the usual information sources, like Facebook and Twitter. The attack had impacts, though, in some places more than others. In most cases, the impact was to create even bigger jams of disabled vehicles, already huge because so many had simply run out of gas without electricity to pump it from the underground tanks.

Electric vehicles, so heavily touted as "better than fossil fuel" were all dead, too. What Barham could not have envisioned, however, was that the OnStar attack might have some positive effects. Like grinding a criminal convoy to a dead halt.

As the New Southie's had made their advances to the north, they were under constant surveillance by Charlie Fernall's Free State Militia. Charlie had every intention of attacking the convoy of "massholes" as he called them and had picked a spot for the ambush. He needed every advantage he could get because his own troops were spread thin, trying to collect more resources and members from the residents from the Lakes region and the Mt. Washington Valley area. There were estimated to be over two hundred of the marauders calling themselves 'The New Southies,' and only fifty or so militia members available to fight them. Not terrible odds, the former Marine thought, but not great.

Once the invaders robbed Sig Sauer, the dynamics shifted. They were now tenfold better armed than the militia, and they had new vehicles with plenty of fuel. Head-to-head fighting would not be pretty, Charlie knew. But his ambush plans would give him the upper hand. There was a stretch of Route 16 alongside Lake Chocorua that was perfect.

The road went up a steep hill with a blind curve at the top. Beyond the crest, the road narrowed with a steep hillside bank on one side and the lake on the other. Charlie would block the road beyond the crest of the hill and then, once the convoy passed the junction of Route 113, he would also block the road behind them. A classic kill zone. His people were ready. But like most battle plans, things did not go as expected.

"Boss," said the voice on the radio, "something weird going on down here." The call was from one of Charlie's scouts, positioned further south. "Their vehicles just went dead."

"What the fuck?" asked Charlie. "All of them?"

"Hard to say, sir. Most of them, for sure. All the lead vehicles – the new ones, looks like — and some others. They are all out cussin' and looking under the hoods. They were cruisin' along at about sixty, then just rolled to a stop."

Charlie heard a commotion behind him.

"What the hell's wrong with my damn truck?" someone shouted. "Fuckin' thing just died!"

Several other shouts of "Mine, too!" and "Here, as well!" rose up from his crew.

Charlie Fernall pushed the starter button on his F-150. It fired right up. The Ram 3500 next to him was also running, as was Bill Davison's Toyota Tundra. Only the Chevy's, he thought. Fucking strange.

"Can you tell which of their rides are shut down?" Charlie asked his scout. "And are they able to continue?"

"From what I can see, it's mostly the GMs they just stole, down in Exeter. I can see a few Fords and others that seem to work. All the new ones were up front, though. Probably driven by their mucky-mucks. Those are blocking the north-bound lane from shoulder-to-shoulder. I think they'll be here for a bit. We should hit them while they're stalled out and confused."

Charlie loaded up half of his troops into the vehicles that were working and headed south. His scouts had told him the best route to follow to mount the best attack on the stalled invaders. Twenty minutes later, the small contingent of the Free State Militia were in position to attack the convoy from the rear.

It was disastrous.

The New Southies were better organized than Charlie had expected. They had fighting discipline that could only have come from military experience. Their rear defenses were solid and well-managed. The militia were out gunned and overconfident. Thousands of rounds were fired in the battle and both sides took casualties, but the militia had fewer men and women in the fight. They were forced to withdraw.

As they retreated, Charlie made a call on the HAM radio in his vehicle, using the channel frequency of 146.52 MHz. In 'normal times,' this frequency would be monitored to provide help if a lost camper or hiker needed it. These days, the frequency had become a broadcast channel for every HAM operator in the country.

"Be advised. My Free State Militia just had our asses handed to us. We've slowed these massholes down, thanks to whatever caused their vehicles to stop working, but they are well-armed and determined fighters. They will find a way to keep coming north. If you haven't made preparations, start now. Charlie Fernall, out."

CHAPTER 31

STRANGE BEDFELLOWS

As usual, Ron Rivera was having his 0600 cup of coffee while scouring the web for reliable sources of news. CNN, Fox News, BBC, and Al Jazeera all had functioning websites, though their audiences were significantly reduced. From the perspective of 'reliable,' Al Jazeera was the one Ron put his stock in. All the others needed to be contrasted and compared to filter out the bullshit and political bias. He looked up as Michael entered the war room.

"*Hola, amigo*," Michael said. "Any news fit to print this morning?"

"Lots of headlines about what looks to be an attack on the General Motors OnStar system," Ron replied. "No assignment of responsibility, yet, but the hack disabled cars and trucks from coast-to-coast. It could have been worse. So many vehicles were already dead because they had no fuel, anyway. Still, it adds to the fucked up situation. Al Jazeera thinks it was likely a last-ditch effort from the Iranians. They are probably right.

"Yep. And it sounds like we will be dealing with our friends from the south, sooner versus later. I'm working through some thoughts about all that." It had been over a week since Charlie Fernall and his Free State Militia had had their butts kicked by the Massachusetts horde. "Our boy Charlie had a rough afternoon. We need to be better prepared than he was."

"No doubt in my mind," Ron said. "You always are. From what I'm picking up on the HAM net, folks up here are in need of some guidance. Not much of a choice between crooks who call themselves Free Staters and crooks from Massachusetts. They both want to take what others have."

"See if you can find out whether Chief Carson down at the Fire Department would be interested in meeting. He's always seemed like a straight shooter, and he knows everyone. I've contributed quite a bit of cash and other support to his department, over the years. I think it's time to find out who else we have around us we can depend on."

"Alliances can be good. Or not. I'll get him on the radio net. They monitor a channel, and I'm sure they monitor the 146.52 MHz feed, too. I'll let you know when I set something up."

"Copy that. Any new comms from our dear old 'Tio Juan?'"

"Nope," Ron replied. "My guess is, he's at the bottom of a pile of rubble in Pyongyang. *Así es la vida.*"

"Such is life, indeed, my brother. At least we were able to play them long enough to get ahead of some terrible shit, so that's a plus. I'm going to reach out to Atwood today, too. See if he can give me any intel on the bigger picture."

After a hot breakfast with his family and off-duty staff members, Michael went into his private office for a moment of meditation and to consider his next steps. He had spent years giving speech after speech to audiences on the international, national and local scale, about the importance of planning for as many potential threats as could be imagined.

Small threats and larger threats. Threats that had a high probability of occurring, like floods, storms and, in some areas, earthquakes, and threats that were considered "Black Swan" events. The term was coined back in 2007 by Nassim Nicholas Taleb in his book, The Black Swan: The Impact of the Highly Improbable. They are events that, while rare or unexpected, would be highly consequential and have a significant impact on the effectiveness of emergency preparedness efforts. Michael had absorbed the concepts laid out by Taleb and always tried to consider the 'Black Swan' effect in every plan he'd written since reading the book. Now, he was dealing with an entire flock of the dark birds.

A few years earlier, Michael had given a presentation on preparedness at the Bartlett firehouse. It was well-attended by folks from all over the region, thanks to an article in the local Conway Daily Sun newspaper. The audience was attentive. Heads were nodding. People took his contact information for further conversations. But very few ever actually called him. Fewer still, it now seemed, acted on any of Michael's recommendations. The follow-up article in the local paper read: "Local Prepper Conrad Draws Big Crowd". That pissed him off. He wasn't a fucking 'Prepper.' He was, however, PREPARED. Now, more folks wish they were, too.

Maybe another presentation would be like flagellating a deceased equine, Michael thought. Or maybe folks that were now living without electricity and other basic necessities would actually listen to him. Whichever way it went, he resigned himself to the fact that he had to do it. He was, above all else, a realist. The reality was, he needed to form local alliances if he – or any of the surrounding people — wanted to survive.

Michael hadn't spoken to General Bob Atwood in over two weeks. Based on Ron's daily intel briefings, he knew that the man was swamped and didn't want to add to his load. But he really needed to discuss the current situation inside America. He hoped Atwood would be, as usual, frank and honest with him. He poured another cup of coffee and pressed Atwood's speed dial number on his satphone.

"Well, good morning, Ranger Mike!" Atwood sounded tired, but as friendly and warm as ever.

"Mornin', sir! How go the campaigns?" Michael said.

"Every day is a new clusterfuck, my friend. But we have had a few wins on our side of the scorecard. Sadly, so have they. And by 'they' I mean a broad collection of unmitigated assholes, ranging from lone wolves to well-organized groups of rabble rousers and anarchists. As you know, I've made sure that Ron Rivera is on the distro list of all but the most sensitive of reports. Not that you and he don't have the clearances, but because you don't need to know."

"I get that," Michael said. And he did get it. When he was in the

Army, he'd personally escorted high-ranking brass out of his area for that same reason. If you don't have a NEED to know, you don't GET to know.

"This is a secure line. Let me open the kimono a bit," Atwood said. "We are seeing continual ground attacks against critical infrastructure targets and the technicians trying to restore the damages. Cowardly shit. IEDs and sniper attacks against power line workers, for God's sake. We've also seen platoon-sized actions against government buildings and even entire cities. We've killed many of them, but they just keep coming back for more. Most of the dead appear to be from Latin America, with Eastern Europeans stirred into the mix. Thing is, most were never documented in our immigration systems. Our problem is that we're running out of people to fight back with.

"FERC are sticking to their 2014 projections. The report they created back then estimated that if the outage lasted for twelve months, around ninety percent of the American population almost 300 million people — could potentially die because of starvation, disease, and societal breakdown. We are only a couple of months into this shit. Sadly, the trends don't look good. FEMA and the Corps of Engineers were able to deploy emergency generators for many critical services – hospitals, nursing homes, some of the bigger evacuation shelters – but refueling them is a daily battle. And one we seem to be losing. The major cities are the worst. Spoiled food, people dying because their at-home medical devices have no power. Lord knows how many have been trapped in elevators and such.

"As I said, though, we've had some wins, too. We've struck some totally unexpected alliances with groups we always thought of as part of the problem. No one in DC will admit to it, but much of that success can be tied back to the work you and Ron have done for us."

"How so?" Michael asked. "I've been feeling like we were part of the problem rather than the solution. Our database hack certainly contributed to some bad shit."

"And your ability to analyze what was hacked and to use your imaginations to predict potential targets has helped to stop some bad shit, too," Atwood responded. "Getting ahead of the train attacks was huge for us. Thanks to the unique skills of General Clark Cunningham, we were able to flip a few of those bastards. Once they realized that they'd been played by the North Koreans and Russians, some of them helped to spread the word upstream into their networks of left-wing and right-wing radicals. The outcome was mixed, as you might expect, with some of the groups cheering the outcomes and others pissed off at being duped. Believe it or not, several factions of ANTIFA are now helping us!"

"Well," Michael said, "that's a twist! ANTIFA? Please, tell me more!"

Atwood laughed. "It's crazy, right? Weird as it seems, once several of their local leaders realized they were being manipulated, they wanted to negotiate. The president elected to give them a shot at running parts of the country that, frankly, we just no longer have the resources to control. Seattle, San Francisco, New York, Portland, Chicago – all in the hands of ANTIFA – for now. Hell, man, those places were already as liberal as they could get. They wanted them, now they have them. Frankly, I think it will become a case for 'be careful what you wish for,' but it is what it is.

"Florida, Texas, Alabama, and some of the other states are ignoring directives out of Washington, DC. Not quite a formal 'secession,' per se, but close enough. We don't have enough military left to stop them. We've lost almost 250,000 troops in Korea and things are still hot over there. We've moved all the units we had in Europe there, too. At home… well… we are pretty much out of juice. Local militia units are popping up all over, some to keep the peace and others to exploit the situation.

"We are forming alliances that epitomize the old adage about 'strange bedfellows.' The deal with China topping the list. We were forced to let them have their way with Taiwan to get their cooperation in North Korea. They sweetened the pot by giving us access to their nasal spray-based Covid vaccine – which actually works. It's already been distributed to our troops. As soon as we figure out how to distribute it stateside, we'll attempt to do so. As you well know, we don't exactly have the trust of the people when it comes to anything Covid or anything Chinese."

"Damn," Michael said. "You've been a busy guy. Makes my issues seem trivial. Almost. For those of us down here in the mud, they surely aren't. We're living some of the things you mentioned, particularly the militia piece of it. The only course I can see is to do what you've done on the large scale – form alliances. I'm about to start that locally. God knows that I've tried before. Maybe now folks will actually listen. Folks are waking up to the fact that this is a long-term problem. I'm going to convince people that, like Spock said: 'The needs of the many outweigh the needs of the few.' In the meantime, old friend, I wish you luck. I've always got a place for you, should you need it."

Michael ended the call with General Atwood. He sat in the quiet of his office, reflecting on everything he'd just learned. He thought about the old saying, "may you live in interesting times." People usually attributed the phrase to some old Chinese curse. Though it seemed most appropriate right now, no actual Chinese source has ever been produced, to his knowledge. That didn't make the saying less appropriate. He'd take 'uninteresting times' over 'interesting times,' any day. Sadly, things seemed to become more and more interesting every day.

Still, he had things to accomplish. Michael walked back to the war room and asked Ron to get the fire chief on the radio.

"Chief Carson, Michael Conrad here. I'd like to have a face-to-face chat. Can I meet you at the firehouse in one hour?"

Michael, Tom, and Nick loaded into Michael's 1969 Nissan Patrol for the drive to the firehouse. It was a great vehicle. Only around a thousand of them had been sold in the United States. A rugged four-wheel drive along the lines of a Range Rover, the Patrol had been the go-to choice for militaries in India, South America and the Middle East. The Australian outback dwellers loved it. So did Michael. It was built for neither speed nor comfort, but for reliability. The Rangers all loved its bone-jarring, teeth-rattling ride, too, and never passed up a chance to use it.

"Badass ride!" Nick said. "All we need in this puppy is a mounted 'Ma Deuce,' and we'd be all set!"

The other men laughed at the visual of an ancient beater sporting a Browning M2 fifty-caliber machine gun in the back. Though none of them disagreed. The laughing stopped when they turned into the parking lot of the Bartlett firehouse. There were several dirty pickup trucks in the parking lot. Some of them were flying yellow Gadsden flags from their bumpers — including the truck they recognized as belonging to Charlie Fernall.

"Well, well. Ain't this dandy?" Tom said, jacking a round into his M4 carbine.

Michael stopped the old Nissan several yards from the nearest truck. All three men got out and took defensive positions behind the vehicle. As they did, Chief Carson and Charlie Fernall walked out of the firehouse door, hands raised.

"Easy, Mr. Conrad," said the Fire Chief. "It's all good. I asked Fernall to be here. We all need to figure this shit out. You're safe. No trouble here."

"Where are the people who own these other trucks?" Michael shouted. "Get them all out here. I promise you; you do not want to fuck with me. Make it happen, or we are out."

Charlie spoke into a small radio. A group of men and women came through the firehouse door, hands high, rifles slung across their backs.

"No trouble, Colonel," Charlie said. "Let's call this neutral territory. For what it's worth, you have my word as a Marine."

CHAPTER 32

ALLIANCES

"FUCK THAT ASSHAT, sir," Tom said. "Let's just exterminate these vermin and get back to the hacienda."

"No," Michael said. "You two stay put. Drop any motherfucker that gets cute. I'm gonna stroll on over there and chew the fat with these boys. I'll do my best to refrain from breaking ole Charlie's knees."

As Michael approached, Chief Carson walked forward to meet him, hand outstretched. The two had known each other for several years. Michael had been a strong financial supporter of Carson's department and had participated in several emergency planning sessions. The two men had a great mutual respect. That mutual respect was the only thing saving Charlie Fernall from the ass whipping Michael so desperately want to administer.

"Chief, good to see you," Michael said, taking the man's hand. Turning to Charlie, he said, "Can't say the same for you. But I do believe that you're not a guy to offer your word as a Marine lightly. So, gentlemen, let's hear what's on your mind. Then I'll tell what's on mine."

The three men went inside the firehouse, to the Chief's small office. Michael didn't like the idea of sitting next to Charlie Fernall, but he knew he should, to calm the situation down.

"None of us are old enough to have lived through the Cold War, right?" Michael began. "I've studied it though, during my military career days. The operative word was 'détente.'"

"Détente," Chief Carson repeated. "I know the word, as I'm sure Charlie does, too." Charlie nodded in agreement, but both he and the Chief still seemed confused. "How does it fit, here and now?"

Michael went on to explain. "Stop me if I get too basic. I mean to say that détente describes the improvement of relations between groups that have been at odds or have had tumultuous relations. Kinda like the Free State Militia and, well, everybody. It involves decreasing hostility levels, fostering cooperativity and working to reduce the likelihood of future conflict or escalation. The aim, particularly in our own current situation, is to create a more stable and peaceful atmosphere for all parties involved. Make sense?"

Charlie clearly didn't like the implications of what Michael had said but slowly nodded his head.

"Michael turned to face Charlie directly. "I came down here today to suggest the Chief pull together a meeting of any local folks that want to attend. My plan was to speak to folks about the need for forming an alliance within the community. I wasn't expecting to find you here, Charlie, but I'm glad it turned out that way. We need to get a few things straight."

"Colonel Conrad, I agree wholeheartedly," Charlie said. "Before you say your piece, let me start. I've realized that I've gotten out over my skis – more than a little bit. The Free State Militia, under my leadership, has made huge mistakes. Not the least of which was attacking your compound. I'm sorry. In the beginning, people were intimidated by our size and our reputation. What people missed was that our members, by their nature, are not warriors. The Free State Project members are libertarians. Our primary aim has always been to create a society with minimal government intervention and maximum personal freedom. We are not inherently violent or militant by nature. When the country started to go south, I saw that as an opportunity to establish ourselves as a new model for the future. I went about it in a fucked-up way. The skirmish at your place and the battle with the Massholes from Boston showed us— and anyone else who paid attention— that we don't have the skills or determination to be military leaders. And I'm afraid that's exactly what we are going to need if we are to survive."

Michael was impressed. It takes a big person to admit when they're wrong. Charlie seemed genuinely contrite and apologetic. And, he was right. The way things were heading, based on what he'd learned from General Atwood, banding together — and standing together, if necessary – would be the only way to survive.

"Michael, I'm all in," said Chief Carson. "I'll get the word out to as many people as I can. I know your guy Rivera is a HAM, too. Have him broadcast it. What we need is a leader, sir. I, for one, think you're the best guy for that job."

"First off, thanks for the kind words," Michael said. "But I think we should let the people decide who sits at the head of the table. And I don't think we want to do an open network broadcast about the meeting. We can't control who will hear it. You can be sure that not everyone who does will be on our team. No, let's stick to word of mouth. Charlie, can you have some of your people work with the Chief to get the invitation out?"

The three men decided on an afternoon meeting, in two days. Charlie agreed to help get the word out to the members of the community. They stood, shook hands, and Michael walked back to his team, waiting behind the old Nissan Patrol.

"You ain't gonna believe this shit," he said to Nick and Tom, as he climbed into the driver's seat.

Michael felt good about the direction things were moving. He still didn't like Fernall, but he had a bit more respect for him now. At least including him in the alliance was better than worrying about fighting his poorly organized collection of over two thousand people. What Michael didn't know was, his wasn't the only new alliance being formed.

Ed Flanigan and his New Southies were creating alliances, too. Ever since the word spread about the battle with the Free State Militia, random groups of young men and women had been offering to join up with Flanigan's group. They came from Portsmouth, Manchester, and smaller communities, all wanting to be a part of the "winning team".

Some, if Flannigan thought they were worth a damn, he allowed to join his band of marauders. Others, he ordered executed on the side of the road. His army had grown to almost three thousand well-armed members.

The New Southies included hundreds of veterans, many of whom had been homeless and neglected before the shit hit the fan. Now, they had a sense of purpose. And a sense of belonging. Flanigan used them to train the rest of his ragtag army in military tactics and combat readiness. Anyone who didn't measure up – or wouldn't measure up – were disposed of in very public ways. Those left were motivated, both by the idea of taking anything they wanted – and by fear of Ed Flanigan.

A few of the gaggle were experienced mechanics. It had taken them a week, but they figured out ways to bypass the onboard computer systems affected by the OnStar hack. With their vehicles all back in service, their northward invasion was rolling again.

CHAPTER 33

SETTING THE STAGE

DOING KILLER PRESENTATIONS had always been one of Michael's strong points. He had always been in high demand at conferences all over the world, thanks to his vast amount of real-world experience. The presentation he was about to give, he knew, would be the most important one of his life.

New Hampshire's rural, mountainous regions are known for their independent-minded residents. These areas are sparsely populated and often isolated, and the people who live there are accustomed to relying on themselves for their basic needs. Many were outdoorsmen, farmers or loggers, with a deep connection to the land. They are used to hard work and self-sufficiency, and they often prefer to solve problems on their own rather than relying on outside help. Michael was sure they hadn't acted on his previous advice for all those same reasons. He hoped this time would be different.

Michael searched through his library of presentations, where he found three that he could slice and dice to create a compelling set of messages to deliver to the people of his community. This was bread and butter to him. He tailored every presentation he'd ever done to fit the audience for whom it would be delivered. In this case, his focus was to be impactful without being preachy. Direct, without being insultingly simplistic. It would be a tough crowd and he knew it. He finished the new slide deck as the sun was coming up over the mountains.

"Eagle One, Eagle Four," came Nick's voice over the radio. "Big red truck at the lower gate, sir. Chief Carson, asking to see you."

"Buzz him through, Nick," Michael replied.

Chief Carson was driving his wildland firefighting rig. It was a military surplus Stewart-Stevenson 'deuce-and-a-half' that had originally been an Army medical unit vehicle. Big and rugged, with a raised chassis, it looked like it could go just about anywhere.

"Michael, good morning," the Chief said. "Sorry to roll up on you so early in the day. I've been out all night, visiting the locals."

"All good, Chief. Let's grab a cuppa joe and you can tell me what's happening."

The two men sat in Michael's sunroom, overlooking the Presidential Range. The rising sun was painting the bottom of a stack of giant lenticular clouds a bright pink, making them appear like massive flying saucers about to land.

"Looks like the mothership about to lift us all out of here," Chief Carson said, sipping his steaming coffee. "Right now, I'd be inclined to accept the offer."

Michael laughed. "I hear that," he said. "Gotta say, Chief, it's an amazing view from up here. I never grow tired of it. So, how's it coming along with our project? Are folks buying in?"

"They are, for the most part. It's New Hampshire. Some folks will trust nothing told to them by a person in uniform – and that includes me. Even though I've lived here my entire life. Other folks are still pissed at Fernall and his crew. Most of them paid him off, but none of them enjoyed being bullied into it. Still, I believe we're going to have a good turnout. If it goes well, word will spread, and more will get on board. We're all set for tomorrow afternoon at 1400 hours."

"There's an old saying that no man is a prophet in his own hometown. I'm hoping my reputation will help us get past some of that. I don't know many of the locals, but they know of me, thanks to the articles in the Daily Sun. In other words, I'm not from the government, but I am here to help."

As the men drank their second cup of coffee, Michael shared some of what General Atwood had told him about the goings-on in the rest of the world. The Chief closed his eyes and slowly shook his head.

"We are truly fucked," Carson finally said.

"We could be," Michael agreed. "But we don't have to lay back and wait for the Grim Reaper. We can do what we can do – and that will keep most folks alive." Looking directly into the fire chief's eyes, he said, "But not everyone."

Michael joined his family for breakfast. He filled them in on the upcoming meeting as they ate. Everyone was onboard with his plan and prepared to help as needed. After breakfast, he went to the war room to catch up with Ron.

"Mornin', amigo," Michael said. Anything good – or otherwise – to report?"

"Good morning, sir. Nothing on what's left of the web but the usual boilerplate blather. Unfortunately, one of the local HAMs has been chattering about your meeting tomorrow. A few others have told him to shut the fuck up, but he's still making noise about it. Mostly bitching about the fact that the Free Stater's are involved. You might be in for an interesting afternoon tomorrow."

Michael shook his head. Interesting indeed, he thought. He thanked Ron for the report, patted his pal on the back, and went back to his office to catch a few much-needed winks. The winks turned into nods. The nods turned into the longest sleep he'd had in weeks.

Fourteen hours later, Michael slowly regained entry into the world of the living. He went to his private bathroom, took a long hot shower, got dressed, then walked to the command bunker. It was the middle of the night, but he knew someone would be on duty. He found his son-in-law, Jeff, at the HAM radio desk.

"Kinda late for you, isn't it, sir?" Jeff asked.

"Depends on your point of view, buddy. I just woke up from a near-death nap. Over twelve hours, best I can tell. Closer to fifteen. I'm definitely awake now, though. Mind if I keep you company for a bit?" Michael said, pouring himself a cup of freshly brewed coffee.

"All good by me," Jeff said. "I'm just listening to a couple of idiots chewing the rag on the main channel. You know the guy they call 'Huck?'"

"Jacob Hukzinger," Michael replied. "I know of him, but we've never met. Lives further up towards the notch. He's a Nam vet. From what I've heard, he's as close to a hermit as they come and not exactly a friendly neighbor. Nobody around here associates with him. Nor do they fuck with him. What's he up to on the channel?"

"He's stirring shit about the meeting you're having. Been at it since yesterday. Seems to have a few people who agree with him, too. They'll all be there. With this crap all over the airwaves, it wouldn't surprise me if every nutcase in the north woods shows up."

"No good deed goes unpunished," Michael said. "Carry on, son. I'll catch you later."

The night was clear and cold, with an amazing display of stars in the moonless sky. The walk back to the main house was just what Michael needed, to shake the last sleep-induced fuzziness from his brain. Back in his office, he reviewed the presentation he planned to deliver later that day. Considering what he'd just learned, he felt the need to tweak things a bit, to account for the dissenters he now expected to be larger than he'd thought.

Before he knew it, the black sky lightened to a pale gray. Minutes later, the sun made its appearance over the top of Bear Peak. He recalled a line from Kipling's poem, Mandalay: ... *An' the dawn comes up like thunder outer China 'crost the bay* ... Seems legit, he thought.

CHAPTER 34

NEAR-DEATH BY POWERPOINT

AFTER THE USUAL routines of family greetings, breakfast, and a review of the daily briefing from Ron Rivera, it was time to get everyone who was going down to the firehouse. He had Tom, Dar, and Jack load one of his seventy-inch televisions into a van, along with one of the GoalZero solar generators. The firehouse had a diesel generator, but Michael was all about having a Plan B. The group left for the firehouse two hours before the meeting start-time, in order to get everything set up. When they arrived, he pulled his Rangers aside.

"Shit might get weird today, boys," he said. "No need to ask if ya'll are packing, but keep it discrete. Jack, you figure out which of these people is the guy they call Huck, then get a seat close behind him. Dar and Tom, one of you sits toward the back of the crowd and the other in the middle. If the stuff hits the fan, engage as necessary."

"Hoohah!" the men said in unison.

Michael was set up and ready a full hour before the 1400 hours kick-off time for the meeting. By 1330, the parking lot was filling up with trucks and cars of every description. Few Chevys today, Michael thought, half smiling. Another grand reason to be a Ford guy. Chief Carson was in the lot, directing people to parking spaces. Some attendees came inside immediately, to make sure they got good seats. Many hung by their vehicles, alone or in small groups. Several of those small groups were decidedly not in the best of moods. Moods that seemed to worsen when Charlie Fernall and ten pickups carrying members of the Free State Militia arrived.

Michael walked out to join Chief Carson and the two of them walked towards Charlie's trucks.

"Fernall," Michael began, "you and your crew need to keep your shit together. Look around. You are not the most popular gals at the dance. I'm going to ask you to leave your weapons in your vehicles."

"Good afternoon to you, too, Colonel," Charlie said, grinning. "You've heard of the Second Amendment, right? You think everybody else here is leaving their shit in their rides? They won't, and neither will we. But I'll meet you halfway. We won't carry our long guns. Be advised; we aren't here to cause trouble. We're here to make nice with everyone."

Charlie was right, and Michael knew it. New Hampshire was a constitutional carry state. Even before the world went to hell, most of these people wouldn't go to the mailbox without being armed. Nowadays, most wouldn't take a dump without a sidearm within reach. The only thing Michael could do was play into all that.

At 1355, Chief Carson blasted a short squawk from one of his truck sirens. He had a PA system set up for the presentation. Michel took the microphone and asked everyone to please come inside and get seated. Charlie and his crew of Free Staters sat in the front row of folding chairs, ten feet from the podium. Huck Hukzinger and several of his band were in the row behind them. Jack's seat was two rows behind Huck.

"Good afternoon, neighbors," he began. The crowd muttered a weak "Good afternoon," in response. "For those of you who forgot your weapons, I've asked Chief Carson to make an assortment available to loan out. Please return them with as many rounds in the chamber as were already in them."

That broke the ice, garnering a good round of laughter from most of the people in attendance. Not everyone laughed, though. Huck Hukzinger wasn't even smiling.

Michael stood behind a small podium, using his iPad to deliver the presentation. It was connected to the large screen TV via a Wi-Fi router he'd brought with him. He spoke to the crowd with the confidence and demeanor of a leader.

"Today, I want to discuss with you the significance of creating local alliances. Recent events, particularly the widespread power outages, have shown us that crises can, and usually do, strike without warning. Therefore, it's essential that we begin today to work together for all our survival.

"Long-term power outages cause havoc and chaos – we're seeing that right now. Accessing necessities like food, water and medical supplies are difficult here in our part of the world, but I can tell you for a fact that it's one hundred times worse in the big cities of America.

"I've invited you all here to discuss forming local alliances with our neighbors and emergency agencies because that is the only viable means of ensuring our survival."

Michael looked around the room, taking stock of the crowd. He was pleased to see most of the heads nodding in agreement. Most. He touched his iPad screen, projecting the first slide on the screen. In large letters, the TV screen read:

Preparing for a crisis begins with cultivating trust among our neighbors and community members!

Michael continued to speak. "Trust is paramount to any successful partnership or collaboration, especially during times like these. We can build that trust by sharing resources, being open about needs and capabilities, as well as demonstrating dependability and consistency."

"Bullshit!" came a voice from the front of the crowd. Huck Hukzinger was on his feet. "You talk about trust with this motherfucker sitting here?" he asked, pointing his left forefinger at Charlie Fernall. His right hand was pulling a pistol from the small of his back.

Michael saw Jack move to grab Huck from behind. Not gonna make it, he thought. As Huck's right hand brought the semiautomatic pistol up, Michael used what he had; he sailed his iPad like a Frisbee – or an oversized martial art throwing star — aiming for Hukzinger's face. Direct hit! The one-and-a-half-pound aluminum and glass device caught Huck just below his nose, causing him to jerk backwards, right into Jack's diving lunge. The pistol clattered to the concrete floor of the firehouse.

Charlie Fernall was on his feet, pulling his own pistol, as were his crew and several other people around them. Michael was already in motion. He took one long stride, clearing most of the ten-foot gap. He then executed a jumping front kick to Charlie's back, knocking him off his feet. Michael jumped on top of the former Marine, grabbing him in a rear naked chokehold.

"Stop, Charlie," he said, speaking quietly into the man's ear, "or I'll choke you out."

Charlie relaxed. "The fucker was going to shoot me. That shit don't float," he said.

"We've got him under control. No one, thankfully, fired a shot," Michael said. "If you pull yourself together, we can use this to make our point." Charlie moved his head in what would have been a nod, save for the arm around his throat.

Chief Carson was at the microphone. "Sit the fuck down, all of you!" he shouted.

Jack was dragging Huck Hukzinger out the door of the firehouse. Tom, Dar and about twenty others had their guns trained on the Free Staters, who had their own guns pointed at the crowd. Michael helped Charlie back to his feet.

"Stand down!" Charlie commanded his crew. "It's over."

Michael walked back to the podium and took the mic back from Chief Carson.

"Okay," he said. "Now that we've gotten that out of the way." Nervous laughter rose up from the crowd. "I know that emotions and tensions are high. I also know that many – if not most of you – are not fans of the Free Staters. You probably know that I've had my own run-in with them, too. But I'm prepared to move past that, and you need to do that, too. Charlie Fernall would like to say a few words, then we can get back to our regular scheduled programming. Charlie?"

Fernall walked up to the podium, clearly nervous about speaking before a crowd. "I'm not good at this," he began. "Never did like speaking in front of a group of people. Except for soldiers. Because they have to listen and obey. I'm also shitty at apologies. But I offer you mine, right now. We were wrong – no, I was wrong – in how we went about things. Funny thing is, my goal was about the same as the one we're all here to talk about, today. I wanted to create a strong army. My mistake was in using coercion and conscription instead of asking for cooperation. That wasn't right.

"I've also learned that my band of Free Staters are not warriors. That proved itself out a few miles from here, at the Conrad compound and again down Route 16, where we engaged with the massholes coming this way. What we learned is, Conrad and his crew have their act together. So does the asshole Ed Flannigan and his so-called New Southies. We need to pay attention to what the Colonel is saying here because, I promise you, those massholes following Flannigan are brutal and merciless.

As it stands, I have a couple of thousand people who are still loyal to our libertarian principles but realize that we can't hold on to what we have without help. If you'll have us, we want to be a part of this new alliance that Colonel Conrad is talking about. That's all I've got," he said, handing the mic back.

The crowd was at first silent, then, a smattering of applause started. The applause increased, with people standing up from their chairs.

Michael was smiling. When the crowd quieted down, he continued the rest of his presentation. Thanks to Charlie Fernall's statements, the rest of it was an easy sell.

"Since my iPad has been… ah… 'compromised,' the rest of this will be oral. Here's the deal. I attempted to make a point about developing trust between us as a first step. Without that, none of the rest will work. If we can all leave here with that established, we then need to create our own emergency action plan. I've done plenty of those and will take the lead. It will include a plan for identifying the skills, tools, and resources in our new collective. That means being honest. None of us has everything we will need to get our foundation under us. Some of us have more than others. This is where we begin sharing and taking care of each other.

"We need to quickly establish channels of communication. Some of you, like myself, are HAM operators. I have a couple of extra rigs to share with those that aren't. If anyone else has spare gear, get with the Chief to start a pool. We won't be able to get radios to everyone, so we need to form a 'sneaker net' – getting the word out by actually going to visit your less-equipped neighbors.

"I'd like to establish a list of everyone with military experience. Combat experience will be a plus, but understanding discipline and organization is just as important. Again, get with Chief Carson. That needs to happen ASAP. We have some specific actions to take immediately – things might get hot. For now, raise your hands if you've served."

As Michael expected, about half the people in the room raised their hands. This part of New Hampshire had more than their share of retired military. "Now," he continued, "any combat engineers in the group?"

Four hands stayed up. "You four please see me immediately after this meeting."

Michael had spoken to many large audiences. He could read a crowd. What he saw before him was one that was all-in on his messages.

"In conclusion, we can't predict when another crisis will come along. They seem to be stacked up, right? I do know this, though. By taking these steps we've agreed upon today, we can increase our resilience and preparedness for whatever comes next. Remember: we're all in this together; together we can overcome any challenge. That is all."

CHAPTER 35

PLANNING THE WORK; WORKING THE PLAN

MICHAEL WATCHED AS the veterans gathered around Chief Carson at a small table across the room. The four men who had been engineers walked to the front, along with six other men. One man extended his hand.

"Colonel Conrad, my name is Elliott. Retired O-6 myself. Retired as Commandant of the Army Engineering School at Leonard Wood."

"Hooah, Colonel!" Conrad said. "I went through Basic at Fort Lost in the Woods. Glad to have you with us."

"Yes, sir," Elliott said. "Glad to be here. I know these other young fellows from the VFW. Much more current in the dark art of building shit and blowing shit up than I am. These other boys are local contractors. They have access to excavation equipment, but we seem to be a bit fuel-challenged at the moment. What's your plan, sir?"

Michael introduced himself and shook each man's hand.

"Frankly, my plan is to create a plan with you guys. As I see it, our top priority is to stop – or at least substantially slow – the advance of those 'massholes', as Fernall calls them. Open, head-to-head fighting will be a losing proposition. We need some good old Yankee ingenuity. If you have ideas, let's hear them. As far as the fuel, I can help with that."

Dave Emmet, one of the local contractors, was the first to speak up. "Well, sir, I spent ten years as a Road Agent for the county. I know the roads like the back of my hand. We are in a pretty good location here, with only a few ways in or out. From the south, there are really only two main routes, this time of year: Up highway 16; and over the notch on Route 302. Both of them have spots that could be blocked, with a little time and a lot of explosives. I don't know how much of the first we have, but my boss has a shed full of the second."

The group of men spent the next hour laying out a plan to blast a cliff face, just south of the Mt. Washington Hotel, thereby filling Route 302 with enough granite to stop an armored division. With no such natural barriers available south of them on Route 16, they used excavators to tear up the road, south of the intersection with Route 112 and also to destroy the Saco River Bridge in Conway.

"Excellent plans," Michael said. "Let's get rolling – we don't have enough time to wait for daylight. Take shooters with you. We don't know whether they have scouts this far north, but should assume that they do."

The meeting flowed into the evening. Chief Carson had done a great job of assigning roles and team leaders, including communications, feeding missions, safety, defense and medical. Michael was proud to see that his own family members were first in line to help in each of those sectors.

He also noticed that the rough group that had been with Huck Hukzinger were at the table, too, offering to help. Several had been living 'off the grid' for years and knew methods and systems that would soon become more valuable than gold.

I love it when a plan comes together, Michael thought, channeling his inner "Hannibal Smith". It was going to be a long night, but the energy was high.

CHAPTER 36

EPILOGUE

SIX MONTHS AFTER the planning session at the Bartlett firehouse, a sort of "new normal" had set in for the people of the Mount Washington Valley. The alliance had grown, as the word spread about the benefits being realized by banding together and helping one another to survive. But, as Michael had expected, it was not always easy.

The efforts to close off the roads had worked, but five good men died. One man had simply been in the wrong place when the dynamite brought down tons of granite onto Route 302. The others — including one of his son's-in-law — were shot by snipers while working to destroy Route 16. In the end, however, the New Southies – Michael had never liked the term "massholes" – had directed their attention to the wealthy areas around Lake Winnipesaukee and then south towards Concord and Manchester, back down Interstate 93.

The firehouse had become a hub for collecting and distributing resources of every kind. Gasoline for cars and trucks was scarce, but cars were everywhere. Their batteries were scavenged and then put into a rotating pool to ensure that people with critical medical devices could keep them going. Anyone with solar panels on their homes donated one or two in order to keep the batteries charged. Crude wind and hydro generators were crafted too, for the same purpose.

Michael's family and crew were fully engaged. The two nurses had teamed with others from the community to establish a functional medical center. Andrea and Alison were in their elements, organizing events and setting up procedures for everything from entertainment for the children to pot luck dinners for everyone. Larry and B had established eye care and veterinary services for any who needed them, along with chipping in on anything else that needed doing.

Dar, Jack, Tom, and Nick had formed a strong defense force, training them in the skills that Rangers were the best in the world at performing. They had turned the loose-knit group of locals into a formidable, organized fighting force. They all expected to need that, eventually.

The old-timers who'd spent years living off-grid were a treasure trove of information and knowledge. They had books on techniques for building systems for everything from capturing rainwater to building animal and fish traps.

In the first meeting after the formation of the alliance, Michael was appointed as leader. They wanted to call him "Mayor", but he refused. "Michael will do just fine," he'd said.

Ron Rivera maintained HAM radio contact with the outside world. Reports were generally dire, but there was occasional good news. He heard of other resilient groups, much like they'd formed, holding their own. The cities, though, were not much more than post-apocalyptic wastelands.

During his morning meditation sessions, Michael wondered whether the world he'd known would ever recover. His confidence was low. He now had a new mantra: "One day at a time…"

AFTERWORD

Whoa. That was a lot, right? What you've just read is a work of fiction. More like a dramatization, really, because everything I've written about is possible. Some of it could happen tomorrow. Some of it is happening right now.

I've spent the past twenty-plus years working in the world in which my protagonist, Michael, lives. Disaster response, crisis management consulting, emergency planning, refugee shelters, undocumented migrant shelters, social upheavals, chemical spills, biological crises. I've seen all that from an insider's perspective.

It was not, therefore, much of a stretch to game out the "what if...?" scenarios that make up the story you've just read. Frankly, many of my real-world experiences have been so surrealistic that most readers would write them off as impossible.

They clearly were possible because I lived through them. As are the scenarios in this book. In this section, I hope to show you why this is true. After I share some interesting facts – nothing secret; all in the public domain — I'll offer you some tips and ideas on how you can be better prepared for whatever may come.

I start the novel with a description of The Great Eastern European Exodus. Could that happen, you wondered? Well, I believe it could. Here's why. Zaporizhzhia is among the top ten nuclear power plants in the world and is the largest in Europe. The six light-water nuclear reactors were built by the Soviet Union in 1980.

But Hamish de Bretton Gordon, the former head of the Chemical,

Biological, Radiological, and Nuclear Defense Forces (CBRN) in the British Army and NATO, says that it's not only about the reactors.

De Bretton-Gordon stated that the area surrounding the plant contains silos of radioactive waste. The soil around these silos could emit radiation if it is disturbed. He said that if the contaminated material caught fire or exploded, it would not be limited to Ukraine. It is likely that it will affect the entirety of Europe, and Russia too.

Juan Matthews, a visiting professor of the Dalton Nuclear Institute of the University of Manchester in Britain, said that if a large enough accident occurred, it would have serious consequences for the people of the Ukrainian Black Sea Port of Odesa as well as "people from Romania, Bulgaria and Turkey."

Depending upon the severity of the disaster and the prevailing winds etc., the total number of people who could be affected total almost one billion. Even if only a limited number initially died, the panic would lead to a mass exodus from the countries affected. This would be a humanitarian nightmare for the world.

I went on to play out a scenario around insider threats and social engineering, featuring my character, Raúl Hernandez. For a bit of background, I've been an information technology professional for over forty years. Much of that time was specifically focused on cybersecurity – even before the word became a "term of art".

I've served as an executive in some of the most prestigious advisory services companies, providing guidance to hundreds of top-tier organizations whose names you would know. I continue to advise companies on the risks of cyber-attacks, and on how to handle them when – not if – they occur.

You saw Raúl, working from the inside of Michael's company to give access to very bad actors. Those bad actors then took the data they exfiltrated and used the information to penetrate even more organizations.

In a report from the prestigious Ponemon Institute, they state:

External attackers aren't the only threats modern organizations need to consider in their cybersecurity planning. Malicious, negligent and compromised *users are a serious and growing risk. As the 2022 Cost of Insider Threats: Global Report reveals, insider threat incidents have risen 44% over the past two years, with costs per incident up more than a third to $15.38 million.*

Data breaches have become an increasing worry for organizations worldwide, threatening both financial and reputational damage. Insider threat-driven data breaches are especially dangerous as they come from within an organization and thus make it harder to detect and prevent than external attacks. As with my character Raúl, factors contributing to insider threat dangers include:

Authorized access: As insiders have legitimate access to sensitive data and systems, they have access to circumvent security measures that would otherwise thwart external attackers — making it easier for them to exfiltrate data or cause damage.

Knowledge of internal processes: insiders have an intimate knowledge of an organization's operations, security protocols, and weaknesses — giving them an edge when trying to hide their tracks or commit fraudulent acts. With such knowledge in hand, it becomes more difficult for outsiders to detect these activities and prevent further misdeeds by insiders.

Malicious intent: disgruntled employees or contractors could release sensitive information intentionally as a form of revenge or for personal gain, to sabotage an organization's systems.

But what happens with the stolen data? As depicted in this novel, stolen credentials are often put to further nefarious uses. Social engineering techniques are used by attackers to coerce people into divulging sensitive information or performing actions that compromise security. They are made more successful by using stolen credentials to gain entry into target organizations.

Attackers can exploit trust by impersonating legitimate employees or contractors and use this to bypass security measures and gain access to sensitive data.

We saw the triumvirate use stolen credentials to craft targeted spear-phishing emails that appear from known and trusted sources. These highly tailored spear-phishing attacks provided access to systems belonging to their target organizations, through malicious links or attachments in emails. Once inside, the hackers have free rein to create havoc or steal even more data.

Like Robert Watkins in the story, attackers might use stolen credentials to impersonate authorized employees, gaining physical access to sensitive or secure areas.

Now, let's move on to the refugee / migrant shelters. I feel uniquely qualified to discuss this topic, as I have been personally involved with every phase of designing, building, and operating these facilities since 2014. My work has included housing adults and unaccompanied children who've crossed the southern borders of the USA, and other facilities housing refugees from Afghanistan and Ukraine. Tens of thousands of people. I performed these duties under contract to three different presidential administrations. The work stayed the same, regardless of the party in control of the country.

Mandatory detention was officially authorized by President Bill Clinton in 1996, with the enactment of the Antiterrorism and Effective Death Penalty Act (the Act gave the Attorney General discretion to extend detention) and the Illegal Immigration Reform and Immigrant Responsibility Act. The number of shelters / detention facilities has increased every year since.

By the end of 2021, apprehensions hit levels not seen in twenty years. Over 1.5 million people arrived at the border and crossed for the first time in that year alone. At the end of fiscal year 2022, Customs and Border Protection (CBP) had arrested 2,150,370 illegal immigrants attempting to cross the southern border.

While the number cannot – for obvious reasons – be fully known, it's reported that over 900,000 more are what's known as "gotaways" – as the moniker implies, these were people who were not captured by the CBP. That number is for fiscal year 2022 alone. Since 2020, the number is estimated to be over two million.

Citizens of over one hundred non-Latin American countries have been detained at the southern border. Over one hundred and fifty detainees are on the FBI Terrorist Watchlist.

I've been up close and personal with thousands of these immigrants. Most are decent, honest people who are simply trying to make a better life for themselves and their families. Most of those either follow the rules for applying for asylum or simply turn themselves in after illegally crossing the border. But what about the millions who don't get apprehended? What if…?

A reliable source for those who wish to learn more is the Washington Office on Latin America (WOLA). WOLA is a leading research and advocacy organization advancing human rights in the Americas. They produce a regular report on the issues and status of migration at the US southern border.

https://www.wola.org/2023/03/weekly-u-s-mexico-border-update-reduced-february-migration-2024-budget-ciudad-juarez-incident/

Now, let's look at the issue of fentanyl. In fiscal years 2021 and 2022, over twenty-five thousand pounds of fentanyl were seized at the southern border of the United States. Over fourteen thousand pounds in 2022 alone. We have no realistic way of knowing the quantities that actually made it past our hard-working agents, even with their advanced scanning and detection systems.

Based on their recent reports, The Drug Enforcement Administration's (DEA) Washington Division seized over 8.3 million potentially deadly doses of fentanyl in 2022.

https://www.dea.gov/press-releases/2023/01/26/dea-washington-division-announces-seizure-over-8-million-deadly-doses

You can do your own math to see the numbers for previous years.

In this novel, I describe a scenario wherein fentanyl is used as a Weapon of Mass Destruction (WMD) in the hands of a terrorist. If you don't think that's a realistic threat, here's some information for you:

As early as the 1990s, the United States Department of Defense (DOD) recognized the potential of fentanyl for use as a battlefield incapacitation agent but failed to resolve the "margin of safety" problem prior to terminating the program. The margin of safety is the difference between dosages that incapacitate a person and those that kill them.

This difference, or margin, varies from person to person. It is impossible to know if a dose that is powerful enough to incapacitate reliably a population target will also kill a large percentage of the population unless there is a sufficiently large margin. DOD has never weaponized fentanyl, but at least one other country has.

In October 2002, Russia used fentanyl analogs in an act of counterterrorism. Forty Chechen terrorists took over the Dubrovka Theater in Moscow, along with 800 hostages. They strung explosives all around the theater and threatened to destroy the building and kill hostages unless Russia agreed that its military campaign against Chechnya would end.

After several days without success, and with the Chechens threatening to start killing hostages, the Russian security forces used an aerosolized mixture of two fentanyl analogs to paralyze the residents and allow the building to be stormed. About 130 hostages and terrorists were killed. The majority of hostages were killed by exposure to lethal doses of fentanyl compounds.

This would appear to answer the question whether fentanyl-containing compounds could be used to create a WMD. Is it possible that an enemy would use fentanyl as a weapon to kill a large number of people? That's a more difficult question to answer.

It's reasonable to conclude that there are fentanyl-based compounds that could be used as weapons. It's also mind boggling to think that over eight million (remember, that's how much was SEIZED, not how many actually found its way to the streets) lethal doses of the stuff could be consumed by even the most addicted in our country. Where's all the rest of it going?

What if…?

https://wmdcenter.ndu.edu/Publications/Publication-View/Article/2031503/fentanyl-as-a-chemical-weapon/

Are you seeing a trend here?

So, let's address the power grid. I've been pounding my shoe on the table about grid vulnerabilities, for two decades. I served as an anti-terrorist consultant to BC Hydro, in preparation for the Vancouver Olympics, in 2010. I've provided consulting and technical services to

The New York Power Authority, Carolina Power and Light, and Duke Power. I've spoken on the topic at major conferences. It scares the hell out of me.

As a risk management professional, I look at threats with a view towards two factors: probability of occurrence; and impact of an occurrence. Sadly, the US power grids rank high in both categories. Setting aside the more complicated – but most impactful – scenarios of a major solar flare, or a nuclear electromagnetic pulse (EMP) event, our grid is still at considerable risk. Here's a blog post that I recently added to my website:

The United States power grid is an intricate and interconnected network that supplies electricity to homes, businesses and industries throughout the nation. While essential to modern life, its functioning remains vulnerable to various threats including cyberattacks, physical attacks, natural disasters and aging infrastructure. This blog post will discuss these vulnerabilities and the potential consequences arising from them.

Cybersecurity Threats

Cybersecurity threats to the US power grid remain a primary concern, with sophisticated cyberattacks capable of leading to widespread power outages, economic disruption and even loss of life. Recent events, such as SolarWinds cyber-attack, illustrate foreign adversary intrusion into critical infrastructure networks posing significant danger. Some potential categories for potential grid security threats can include:

Advanced Persistent Threats (APTs): Advanced Persistent Threats (APTs) are cyberattacks orchestrated by well-funded and highly skilled adversaries, often state sponsored. Such attacks often include long-term reconnaissance activities and covert intrusion to gain access to sensitive systems with potential to cause extensive damage to power grids.

Ransomware attacks involve the encryption of an organization's data and demanding payment in return for decryption keys; such attacks have increased significantly and can result in significant operational disruption and financial losses for power grid operators.

Insider threats: Employees or contractors with access to sensitive systems who become disgruntled can pose a significant cybersecurity threat; they could have both the knowledge and ability to cause significant harm from within an organization.

Here's a link to a Forbes article about the cyber risks: https://www. forbes.com/sites/chuckbrooks/2023/02/15/3-alarming-threats-to-the -us-energy-grid--cyber-physical-and-existential-events/?sh=3c5a40101a1e

Physical Attacks

Attacks on power grid infrastructure can cause devastating disruption, as evidenced by the 2013 Metcalf Sniper Attack, which revealed critical substations as vulnerable points for physical attacks. Potential physical threats to the grid include:

Sabotage: Attacks against transformers, substations or other critical infrastructure could lead to power outages and lasting damage, with coordinated attacks aimed at multiple locations having potentially dire repercussions. Physical attacks on the US power grid rose last year by 71%, compared to 2021 and surpassed 2020 figures by 20%. The industry's preeminent clearinghouse predicts the number of serious incidents will continue to rise this year.

According to a leaked confidential analysis of physical attacks on the US power grid authored by the Electricity Information Sharing and Analysis Center (E-ISAC), a data center documenting threats against the electrical system and a division of the North American Electric Reliability Corporation (NERC). In the analysis, E-ISAC "assesses with medium confidence that the recent uptick in serious physical security incidents is likely to continue into 2023 based on the number and nature of recent attacks combined with the overall current heightened threat environment." More can be read here: https://www.cbsnews.com/news/physical-attacks-on-power-grid-rose- by-71-last-year-compared-to-2021/

Theft and vandalism: Copper wire theft has the potential to disrupt operations and damage infrastructure, while vandalism causes less severe harm but may still disrupt grid operations and result in damage or delays in service provisioning.

Aging Infrastructure

Much of the United States' power grid infrastructure is outdated, with components dating back to the early 20th century. Aging infrastructure becomes more susceptible to failure over time and poses greater risk of power outages and reduced resilience; key aging infrastructure concerns include:

Obsolete equipment: Outdated equipment may be less efficient and more prone to failure, while lacking modern cybersecurity measures making it vulnerable to cyber-attacks.

Limited capacity: As electricity demand continues to increase, existing infrastructure may struggle to keep up, leading to outages or inefficiencies that disrupt service locally.

Budget restrictions and competing priorities have led to deferred maintenance on critical infrastructure, increasing the risk of equipment failure and decreasing grid reliability.

Vulnerabilities Within Supply Chains

Supply chains used by power grid operators may expose components and equipment used in their power system to vulnerabilities.

Here are a couple of interesting reports on the topic of risks to our power grid:

- *https://protectourpower.org/2020-cyber-risk-report.pdf*
- *https://www.nerc.com/pa/RAPA/PA/Performance%20Analysis%20DL/NERC_SOR_2022.pdf*

In this novel, I describe an attack on the power grid through use of Internet of Things (IoT). Reality or a figment of my overactive imagination? Sadly, I'm not alone in recognizing this threat:

- https://www.princeton.edu/~pmittal/publications/blackiot-usenix18.pdf

In their report, the researchers state: *We demonstrate that an Internet of Things (IoT) botnet of high wattage devices—such as air conditioners and heaters—gives a unique ability to adversaries to launch large-scale coordinated attacks on the power grid. In particular, we reveal a new class of potential attacks on power grids called the Manipulation of demand via IoT (MadIoT) attacks that can leverage such a botnet in order to manipulate the power demand in the grid.*

I've been in places where long-term power outages were caused by natural disasters. New Orleans, post Katrina; Haiti, after the massive earthquake in 2011; Puerto Rico, after Hurricanes Irma and Maria; Panama City, Florida, after Hurricane Michael; Galveston, after Hurricane Ike. The list goes on. After four days, things get ugly. People die. Social fabric begins to break down.

In a testimony before Congress, Dr. Peter Vincent Pry, then the Executive Director of Task Force on National and Homeland Security, a Congressional Advisory Board dedicated to achieving protection of the United States from electromagnetic pulse (EMP), cyber-attack, mass destruction terrorism and other threats to civilian critical infrastructures on an accelerated basis, made the statement that a long-term (one year) grid blackout could kill up to ninety percent of Americans through starvation, disease, and societal collapse and cause failures of communications, transportation, banking and finance, food and water infrastructures; all necessary to sustain modern society and the lives of 310 million Americans.

Dr. Pry died in August 2022. Here's a link to his full statement:

- https://oversight.house.gov/wp-content/uploads/2015/05/Pry-Statement-5-13-EMP.pdf

Dr. Pry was speaking about an EMP or Solar event. But, if it happened, would you really care what caused it?

I'll close this with links to a few "must read" and "must watch" books and documentaries, and a final question: ***what if...?***

- https://griddownpowerup.com/ — a new and compelling documentary about the vulnerability of our power grid
- https://a.co/d/4phbOXW — in "Lights Out", Journalist Ted Koppel reveals that a major cyberattack on America's power grid is not only possible but likely that it would be devastating, and that the United States is shockingly unprepared.
- https://a.co/d/eqUvwtL — John Matherson's One Second After has already been cited on the floor of Congress as a book all Americans should read, a book already being discussed in the corridors of the Pentagon as a truly realistic look at EMP — a weapon with the awesome power to destroy the entire United States, literally within one second. It is a weapon that the Wall Street Journal warns could shatter America.

WHAT ARE YOU DOING ABOUT IT?

"Dad, my friends think you're a Prepper."

"I'm not a Prepper, son, but I am prepared!"

That was an actual dialogue. That's my story, and I'm sticking to it. But how about you, dear reader? What's your story? Are you prepared?

The beauty of a work of fiction is that the writer can take certain liberties with the facts. That's why they're called "thrillers", right? I wrote the afterword you've just read to show you just how real things could become. Most of the issues addressed in that last section, and which are dramatized in the novel, can be prepared for.

Some are even actionable on your part. You can write letters to your representatives, encouraging stronger and more defined actions on immigration, drug smuggling, and critical infrastructure protection. No voice should go unheard on these important topics. But while you are thinking globally, you should act locally.

In the business of emergency planning and disaster preparedness, we have a saying, "every disaster is local". It's unlikely that you, as an average citizen, can do much to prevent a major catastrophe, regardless of its nature. I've often said, "a hurricane is the only disaster that you can see coming." That said, I never cease to be amazed at how many people see them coming, yet still do nothing to prepare themselves.

Don't be that kind of person.

If we can agree that none of us knows exactly "what" the next major crisis will be, nor "when" that crisis might occur, let's also agree that taking at least basic steps toward preparedness is a good thing.

"I'm not worried. If the shit hits the fan, FEMA will be there to help!" I've heard it a thousand times, and I say for the thousandth and first time: BULLSHIT!

FEMA is NOT a rescue agency. Period. Whatever the bad thing is from a major snowstorm to a hurricane, an earthquake to a terrorist attack, a massive power outage to a pandemic — YOU need to be prepared to take care of yourself and your family. It is your responsibility and no one else's.

If only one person who reads these words actually acts upon them, I will have done my duty to humanity. That one person will be better prepared to SURVIVE.

Let's start from the basics: you need a personal and/or family emergency preparedness plan. It is essential to ensure the safety and well-being of yourself and your family during natural disasters, pandemics, power outages, or other emergency situations. There are great resources for developing such a plan, which I'll direct you to, but I am also providing a solid framework, right here.

This plan outlines steps to take, supplies to gather, and resources to consult to be better prepared for a variety of emergencies, regardless of their nature.

Most of this comes from publicly available sources. Some of the guidance is based on my first-hand, boots-in-the-mud experience, gained through living through some of the largest and most impactful disasters of our lifetime.

Supplies and Materials

Based on recommendations from the Federal Emergency Management Agency (FEMA), American Red Cross, and Centers for Disease Control and Prevention (CDC), the following supplies should be included in your emergency preparedness kit:

- Water: At least one gallon of water per person per day for a minimum of three days (Minyard recommends at least one week!)

- Take this one further. Water, as you know, is the elixir of life. Consider investing in a Berkey water filtration system. It requires no power and will make pure water from virtually any source.
  - www.usaberkeyfilters.com
- If that doesn't work for you, at least invest in several Life Straws. They offer similar filtration.
  - https://lifestraw.com/?gclid=EAIaIQobChMI15b cnJux_gIV2iazAB2IkAKqEAAYASAAEgJHdvD_BwE
- Food: A minimum of a three-day supply of nonperishable food items for each person (FEMA). Minyard says, think ahead!
  - In most situations, three days could be enough. I've seen much, much longer. Consider investing in easy to store, long lasting emergency food, such as available from 4Patriots.
    - https://4patriots.com
- First aid kit: Bandages, gauze, adhesive tape, antiseptic wipes, tweezers, scissors, pain relievers, and a digital thermometer (American Red Cross)
  - Consider the long term. Take a first aid course and a CPR / AED course. Invest in an AED.
    - https://a.co/d/ajCcBYo
  - Get a real medical kit. Look at products from MFASCO or Dark Angel.
    - https://a.co/d/dBk5bqB
    - https://darkangelmedical.com/d-a-r-k-explorer-kit/
- Medications and medical supplies: A seven-day supply of prescription medications, as well as nonprescription medications such as pain relievers, antacids, and allergy medications (CDC). Seven days of medicine but only three days of water? Hmmm...
  - Minyard says consider more of your prescription meds. The other stuff will be in the kits I recommended, but verify that you have enough for everyone for at least a few weeks.

- Personal hygiene items: Toilet paper, soap, hand sanitizer, toothbrushes, toothpaste, feminine hygiene products, and diapers if necessary (CDC).
  - Remember 2020? Stock up before you need it. No need to horde more than you need, but have enough on hand to weather the initial rush. You've already seen how things can go.
- Clothing and bedding: A change of clothing for each person, including warm layers, sturdy shoes, and rain gear, as well as blankets or sleeping bags (FEMA).
  - Have several resilient, easy to wash items.
- Tools and equipment: A battery-powered or hand-crank radio, flashlights, extra batteries, a multi-purpose tool, a manual can opener, and a whistle (FEMA).
  - Consider investing in rechargeable batteries and a solar battery charger
  - Knives – more than one, for different purposes
  - Solar garden lights. Charge them all day and use then at night. Darkness sucks in a disaster. Light is your friend.
- Communication and documentation: A fully charged cell phone with a backup power source, a list of emergency contact numbers, and copies of important documents such as passports, driver's licenses, and insurance policies in a waterproof container (FEMA).
  - If the cell towers remain operational, that is. I've personally lived through situations wherein cell service was virtually nonexistent for over a month or longer. If you can afford to do so, consider investing in an iridium satphone solution. They aren't cheap but could save your life.
    - https://www.satphonestore.com/tech-browsing/satellite-phones/iridium-go.html?gclid=EAIaIQobChMI7rTeqKax_gIVuWxvBB0wVgyDEAAYAyAAEgKPgfD_BwE

- Cash and coins: A small amount of cash and coins for emergency use, as ATMs and credit card machines may be unavailable during disasters (CDC)
  - In most cases, these machines will be useless. Cash is king.
  - Bartering has saved me on several occasions. Even if you don't smoke, tobacco is valuable for trading. As is alcohol, chocolate, gold, and small caliber ammunition.
- Pet supplies: Food, water, medications, and a carrier or leash for each pet, as well as vaccination records and contact information for your veterinarian (FEMA).
- Firearms: I recognize that this is a touchy subject for some, but it needs to be mentioned here. I'm not talking about "assault weapons" (whatever that means). I'm talking about firearms for self-defense and for hunting.
  - Like it or not, you may need a weapon. If you do choose to arm yourself, get ahead of the game – get some proper training! I'm a strong proponent of gun owners knowing what they're doing. Even driver's licenses have to be renewed, after all.
    - Handguns: Don't get more than you can handle. Taking a good training course will help you to figure out what that means.
    - Long guns: You do not need an AR-15 or AK-47 for home defense. Sure, they're cool and all, but a better option is a well-made .12-gauge pump shotgun. Few things will cause a bad actor to break out in a cold sweat like the sound of racking a shell into a shotgun. Bonus: you can hunt with it, too!
    - Small caliber rifle: a good .22 rifle will be a great addition to the kit. Small game is easier to find than big game.
    - Plenty of ammo: for shooting and for bartering
- Backup power: Without electricity, your world will deteriorate quickly. Plan ahead. If you can, consider alternatives to fossil-fuel

generators, such as solar. At minimum, consider systems such as the ones listed below, from GoalZero or Renogy. Gas-operated generators are also a good choice as long as you have a reserve of fuel and follow all the appropriate safety guidelines. A whole-house solution is the best solution, regardless of whether you choose solar or fossil-fuel systems. An automatic transfer switch isn't required, but certainly advisable.

- GoalZero—https://www.goalzero.com/pages/home-energy-storage
- Renogy — https://www.renogy.com/applications/home/

Emergency Plan

- Create a communication plan, including designated meeting spots and emergency contact numbers.
- Establish evacuation routes and practice them with your family.
  - Make sure that every family member has a "Get Home" bag in their vehicles at all times!
  - A Get Home bag is a short-term survival kit, typically stored in a backpack for ease of transport. Its function is to provide you with the basic tools of life should you have to evacuate a home or place of work quickly during an emergency, like a large-scale natural disaster.
    - https://www.bugoutbagbuilder.com/learning-tutorials/bug-out-bag?gclid=EAIaIQobChMInLfw3q-x_gIVZGxvBB01KQl9EAAYAiAAEgJhYvD_BwE
- Learn about local hazards and emergency plans for your community.
- Teach family members how to shut off utilities such as gas, water, and electricity.
- Make sure all family members know how to call 911 and when to use it.
- Regularly review and update your emergency preparedness plan.

REFERENCES

FEMA (2021). Build a Kit. Retrieved from https://www.ready.gov/kit
American Red Cross (2021). First Aid Kit. Retrieved from https://www.redcross.org/get-help/how-to-prepare-for-emergencies/anatomy-of-a-first-aid-kit.html
CDC (2021). Personal Needs. Retrieved from https://www.cdc.gov/disasters/planforpoweroutage.html

To further enhance your family's preparedness for emergencies, it's beneficial to study prepper handbooks and survivalist guides. These resources cover a wide range of topics, from off-grid living to self-sufficiency during prolonged power outages. Here's a list of reputable handbooks and guides to consider:

- "The Prepper's Pocket Guide: 101 Easy Things You Can Do to Ready Your Home for a Disaster" by Bernie Carr This guide offers practical tips and checklists for preparing your home and family for various emergency scenarios.
- "SAS Survival Handbook: The Ultimate Guide to Surviving Anywhere" by John 'Lofty' Wiseman This comprehensive guide, written by a former SAS soldier, covers essential survival skills and techniques to help you in any situation.
- "The Disaster Preparedness Handbook: A Guide for Families" by Arthur T. Bradley, Ph.D. This handbook provides a step-by-step approach to creating a customized disaster preparedness plan for your family.

- "When the Grid Goes Down: Disaster Preparations and Survival Gear for Making Your Home Self-Reliant" by Tony Nester This book focuses on how to make your home self-reliant during a prolonged power outage, including alternative energy sources, food storage, and water purification.
- "The Encyclopedia of Country Living: The Original Manual for Living off the Land & Doing It Yourself" by Carla Emery This extensive guide covers various aspects of self-sufficient living, from gardening and animal husbandry to preserving food and handcrafting household items.
- "The Off-Grid Solar Handbook: A Beginner's Guide to Energy Independence" by Joseph Burdick and Philip Schmidt This guide provides an introduction to off-grid solar power systems, explaining how to design, install, and maintain a solar-powered electrical system for your home.
- "Bushcraft 101: A Field Guide to the Art of Wilderness Survival" by Dave Canterbury This guide offers practical advice on essential outdoor survival skills, such as fire-making, shelter-building, and navigation.
- "The Forager's Harvest: A Guide to Identifying, Harvesting, and Preparing Edible Wild Plants" by Samuel Thayer This book teaches you how to identify, harvest, and prepare edible wild plants, increasing your self-sufficiency during emergencies.

Remember to carefully review and evaluate the information provided in these guides, adapting their recommendations to your family's specific needs and circumstances. Regularly practicing survival skills and discussing your emergency preparedness plan with your family will help ensure that you are ready for any situation that may arise.

The most important tip I can give you is: PAY ATTENTION! Many situations are predictable. Along with paying attention, be prepared to ACT when things get dicey. In her book *The Unthinkable – Who Survives When Disaster Strikes – and Why,* Amanda Ripley reveals how human fear circuits and crowd dynamics work, why our instincts sometimes misfire in modern calamities and how we can prepare for inevitable calamities more intelligently.

Lastly, DO NOT BECOME COMPLACENT! I started this novel with the following statement:

Complacency. It's so comfortable. And so easy to accept. It's always there, lurking in the shadows of great successes and long periods of boredom. And complacency is not your friend.

I don't have room to post links to the obituaries of every person killed because they were complacent. Don't be one of those people.

Thank you, from the bottom of my heart. Without you, writing would not be nearly as satisfying.

Stay prepared!

Printed in the United States
by Baker & Taylor Publisher Services